THE LOST LOVE OF ASHFORD MANOR

Blair Keylines

Copyright © 2024

All rights reserved. No part of this publication may be reproduced, distributed, or transmitted in any form or by any means, including photocopying, recording, or other electronic or mechanical methods, without the prior written permission of the publisher, except in the case of brief quotations embodied in critical reviews and certain other non-commercial uses permitted by copyright law.

TABLE OF CONTENTS

The Lost Love of Ashford Manor

[Chapter 1](#)

[Chapter 2](#)

[Chapter 3](#)

[Chapter 4](#)

[Chapter 5](#)

[Chapter 6](#)

[Chapter 7](#)

[Chapter 8](#)

[Chapter 9](#)

[Chapter 10](#)

[Chapter 11](#)

[Chapter 12](#)

[Chapter 13](#)

[Chapter 14](#)

Chapter 15

Chapter 16

Chapter 17

Chapter 18

Chapter 19

Chapter 20

Chapter 21

CHAPTER 1

The manor loomed ahead, a shadow of its former self, as Elena's car crunched over the gravel path. Each crack of stone beneath her tyres matched the uneasy rhythm of her heartbeat. The once majestic structure now stood weary and worn, its faded grandeur stark against the vibrant Scottish countryside. Vines ran along the stone walls, and the stained glass that had once given off a mosaic pattern was now dulled by the effects of time. Although it continued to stand sturdy, the cracked walls and chipped wooden doors gave off the notion that it had been through several generations and several stories, and now Elena was about to become one of them.

The manor stood as a poignant reminder of both the past's elegance and its inevitable decay. The rustle of the grass behind and the squawking of birds could be heard as the wind blew through Elena's hair.

A golden glow was being cast by the setting sun that lit up the manor's high windows and ivy-clad walls, giving the illusion that the building itself was blushing at her arrival. As the last of the sun's rays cast against the building, it almost formed into the shape of a halo.

As she stepped out of the car, the air was filled with a mix of fresh earth and old stone—a scent that spoke of age and stories hidden within the walls. Elena's breath caught in her throat. Despite the neglect, the manor's architecture spoke to her, a silent plea for rescue that she felt deep in her bones. It was as if the building's faded beauty mirrored her own life—once full of promise, now teetering on the edge of ruin.

However, as she approached, the reality of neglect became impossible to ignore. The garden was overgrown, with weeds choking the once-manicured lawns and wild vines creeping up the sides of the building as if trying to reclaim the manor back to nature. The wooden door was weather-beaten, its paint peeling like dry skin, and the brass doorknob tarnished to a dull green.

Elena reached out, her fingers brushing against the cold metal lion's head of the doorknob, feeling the weight of history and the burden of the task ahead. She was here to oversee the restoration of this historic manor, chosen by the Historical Society of Scotland for her expertise in conservation. The manor, rumoured to have been a pivotal site during various historical events, offered a unique challenge—

one that Elena had eagerly accepted.

The offer had come just in time. Elena had lost her job six months ago. Forced to raise her little sister Lily on her own after the death of her parents, she needed to find a job fast to secure both their futures. She had applied for several jobs and had gotten just as many rejections. This offer had come to her in a moment of sheer luck.

As Elena examined the crumbling facade, a voice with a thick Scottish accent called out behind her, "Quite a sight, isn't she?"

She turned to see a burly man approaching, his ginger hair catching the fading sunlight.

"James McAllister," he introduced himself, extending a firm hand. "Structural engineer. Looks like we've got our work cut out for us."

She instantly recognised his name from the report she had received. James McAllister was the project's structural engineer, a burly man with a gentle demeanour and a sharp mind. With over two decades of experience in restoring historic buildings across the UK, James had an intuitive understanding of structural integrity and the challenges posed by aged buildings like the manor. "The foundation and beams are solid, but there's extensive water damage on the second floor," he reported to Elena, his Scottish accent thick and reassuring.

She extended her hand for him to shake. "You have

quite an impressive track record. I look forward to working with you."

James took her hand, brushing his lips across her knuckles with a grin. "Pleasure's all mine." Elena felt a flush creep up her neck—she wasn't sure if it was from his charm or something else.

"Elena Carter. Pleasure to meet you. Any initial thoughts?"

"Well, the foundation seems solid, but we'll need to address that water damage pronto," James replied, his eyes already scanning the building with practised scrutiny.

As the door creaked open, a draft of musty air rushed to greet her, carrying with it the faint, almost forgotten smells of old books, wax polish, and a trace of lavender. Stepping inside, Elena felt as though she were stepping back in time. Her eyes adjusted to the dim interior, noting the grand staircase winding upwards, the faded tapestries hanging from the walls, and the thick layer of dust that seemed to blanket everything.

"Hello?" Elena called out cautiously.

"The other team members must be somewhere. I will go to find them," James proposed.

With a nod, she looked at him, disappearing into the long corridors before examining the entrance room. Her movements were stiff, and her gaze weary. She felt as though she was intruding on someone's home.

She couldn't help but squeal as the door shut closed behind her, and the lights flickered on.

That wasn't creepy at all.

The silence was suffocating, as if the manor itself was holding its breath, waiting for Elena to uncover the secrets buried within its walls. Yet, as Elena moved through the foyer, her footsteps echoing off the marble floor, there was a palpable sense of potential. Each room whispered secrets of days gone by, of laughter and music, of whispers and cries—a symphony of life that once filled these halls. And yet, each room she passed carried the same air of silence. She found it strange that there was no one there; surely, there would be a manorkeeper to show her around.

Her professional eye assessed the decay, noting the sagging beams and the cracked plaster but also recognising the craftsmanship and the enduring strength beneath the neglect. She couldn't help herself. Her passion for history was something that had been instilled in her from a very young age. From the times when her grandfather used to take her to the art museum just outside her town, and when he opened a gift shop near his lakehouse, selling old knick-knacks. He managed to spin a story for each one, and it would have tourists coming in from all over to have a look at them. After her grandfather's death, Elena took it upon herself to carry on their tradition and went on to study history at the university.

This manor was nothing like she had first expected. Every brick, every wood chip carried its own story. It was a conservator's dream: to bring such a place back to its former glory, to peel back the layers of time and reveal the beauty beneath.

Elena's first impressions were a mixture of awe and melancholy, touched by a resolve that was characteristic of her. She was determined to restore the manor, not just to preserve a piece of history, but to bring it back to life, to ensure it stood as a testament to both the past and the future. As the last light of day slipped away, leaving the halls in shadows, Elena felt a chill of excitement—the kind that only a true lover of history knows, standing on the brink of a great discovery.

Elena was excited to see what this journey would unfold for her. She had a feeling that it wasn't only her that would restore the manor, but the manor would be restoring her as well.

As Elena made her way onto the second floor, she passed the left wing of the manor. The echoes of Elena's footsteps were soon joined by other sounds —the voices and movements of the restoration team she was about to lead. One by one, the team members assembled, everybody contributing their distinct skill set and expertise, which is vital for the enormous effort that lies ahead.

I guess I am not alone anymore.

A blonde-haired woman with blue eyes stepped

forward, smiling. "You have already met James. Ignore him. He flirts with anything with a pulse. I am sure he would flirt with Mrs Sheffield if she would let him," the woman said.

Elena looked confused by her statement. She sighed as she explained, "That's the gardener's wife. I am Sophie Tran, by the way. I am excited to work with you."

Sophie Tran, a young and enthusiastic conservation specialist from London, whose expertise in chemical preservation and passion for sustainable practices had quickly made her an indispensable part of the team. Her energy was infectious, and her respect for historical accuracy aligned perfectly with Elena's vision.

"I've already started assessing the wallpapers and fabrics; there's a lot to preserve and even more to restore," Sophie explained, pointing towards her detailed notes and photographs.

She sure is thorough, Elena thought as she took a moment to look through the photos.

Joining them was Aarav Singh, an architect with a keen eye for historical aesthetics and a deep appreciation for Gothic architecture. Born in India and trained in Edinburgh, Aarav brought a fresh perspective to restoration, often merging traditional techniques with modern technology. His rich skin glowed in the low light. Elena watched as he fidgeted with the glasses perched on the bridge of his nose as he avoided eye contact.

"So, Aarav, what's your vision for bringing this place back to life?" Elena asked, nodding toward the sprawling structure.

Aarav adjusted his glasses, a spark lighting up in his eyes as he spread out his blueprints.

"I believe we can preserve the Gothic essence while subtly integrating modern necessities. Imagine hidden supports that maintain the old-world charm but provide modern safety and lighting that accentuates the original architecture without overpowering it."

Elena leaned in, intrigued.

"That sounds ambitious. I like it."

Aarav cleared his throat as he fumbled with his blueprints.

"We need to respect the manor's original design while ensuring it meets today's standards for safety and comfort," he suggested, unfolding his blueprints on a nearby table.

Clara Bennett was the last member of the team, a historian specialising in Scottish heritage, whose knowledge of local history would guide much of the restoration's thematic decisions. Her features were hardened, her hair pulled into a ponytail, and her brown eyes calculating as she leaned against the far wall. Clara's ability to decipher historical documents and her insights into 18th-century Scottish life was crucial in making the restoration work meaningful.

"It's nice to meet you," Elena offered. Clara made no move to approach her.

Elena blinked, thrown off by the chill in Clara's gaze. She tightened her grip on her notebook, forcing herself to remain composed. However, Sophie spoke up. "She is upset because she thinks you stole her job," she explained.

Understanding dawned on Elena, and she felt a knot form in her stomach. She offered Clara a tentative smile, hoping to ease the tension, but Clara's gaze remained icy, her posture rigid and unwelcoming.

As Elena listened to her team, she felt a growing sense of camaraderie and purpose. Each member was not only a professional in their field but also deeply passionate about their work, driven by a shared goal —to restore the manor not just as a building but as a piece of living history.

Gratitude swelled within her; this skilled team was exactly what the manor—and she—needed.

The scope of the project was immense. Beyond the physical restoration of the structure, the team aimed to make the manor a centre for historical education and community engagement. The challenges were daunting: from replacing the roof without compromising its historic character to updating the plumbing and electrical systems discreetly to preserving the fragile frescoes that adorned several ceilings.

Yet, as they gathered around the old oak table in the centre of the hall, pouring over plans and schedules, the air was thick with anticipation and determination. This was more than just a job for each of them; it was a chance to touch history, to learn from it, and to give it a future.

"I believe that I have been lucky enough to have the chance to lead such a passionate team. Without joint efforts, we would not be able to return this space to its former glory. I will have a look around and determine what requires the most work," Elena instructed.

With the team assembled and the project's goals laid out, Elena felt ready to tackle the challenges ahead. Together, they would peel back the layers of decay and neglect, weaving the past and the present to restore the manor's lost glory. As the meeting concluded, the team dispersed, each to their tasks, united by a common mission, and shared excitement for the journey they were embarking on.

After the introductions and brief discussions with the restoration team, Elena embarked on her first thorough walkthrough of the manor. Armed with a flashlight and notebook, she started from the main entrance, her senses alert to every detail.

The grand foyer, despite its faded grandeur, retained hints of its former opulence. The mosaic tiles underfoot, though obscured by years of dust and debris, spoke of a time when the manor buzzed with the footsteps of the elite. Elena noted the intricate patterns and made a mental note to consult with Sophie on the best methods to restore them without causing damage.

As she ventured further, the scale of decay became more apparent. In the drawing room, the wallpaper, once vibrant and teeming with artistic expression, now hung in tatters, its colours bleached by sunlight streaming through broken panes. Elena's flashlight beam caught the glint of a once-glorious crystal chandelier now lying in pieces on the floor beneath its original setting. She paused, envisioning the room in its heyday, filled with music and laughter, now silenced by the passage of time.

We will have to change the wallpaper and replace the restoration beams.

Moving through the corridors, Elena's attention was drawn to the woodwork. The oak panelling along the walls, though suffering from wood rot, showcased exquisite craftsmanship. Each panel told a story of artisan skill, now in desperate need of James' structural expertise to ensure they could be preserved.

Change the wooden panels.

The library offered a different sort of heartbreak. Here, the shelves stood mostly empty, a few forgotten volumes lying scattered, their spines cracked, and pages yellowed. The musty smell of old paper filled the air, a testament to the many stories that had once captivated readers by the fireplace, now cold and filled with ash. Elena pulled out her camera, documenting each angle for further study, her mind already racing with ideas for seminars and readings that could once again fill the space with eager listeners.

She hoped that there would be a way to salvage at least some of the books. There was an endless possibility of what they may contain, and hopefully, her restoration team would be able to keep at least some of it intact.

In the conservatory, the contrast between life and decay was stark. Overgrown plants had taken over the space, their vines creeping along the ironwork, weaving through broken glass panels. This wild intrusion of nature was both a destructive force and a protective embrace, shielding the delicate structure from complete ruin. Elena made a note to explore potential botanical studies that could integrate the conservatory's revival with the local flora.

Clean up the conservatory.

Something told her that there was more to the conservatory that was hidden beneath the clutter and overgrown plants.

As she ascended the grand staircase to the upper floors, the creak of the wood under her steps echoed ominously. Here, the private quarters lay exposed, the personal effects of past inhabitants long since removed or ruined. In one room, a grand four-poster bed frame still stood, its canopy fabric fluttering like ghosts in the breeze from a broken window. This intimate glimpse into private lives paused Elena in her tracks, a reminder of the personal stories woven into the fabric of the manor.

Varnish furniture and change cushions and mattresses.

Her final stop was the attic, where she had been told a surprise awaited. The narrow stairs leading up were less grand and more utilitarian, and the air grew colder as she climbed. When she reached the top, her flashlight revealed the attic's contents: trunks, furniture covered with dust sheets, and, most intriguing, a mysterious pile of letters bound by a faded ribbon. As Elena knelt to examine them, her heart raced with the thrill of discovery. Each letter was a potential key to unlocking the manor's secrets, a tangible link to the past waiting to be explored.

She took the letters into her hand, deciding that she would have to go through them herself later on. Something told her that there was something important contained inside them.

The walkthrough not only solidified the magnitude of the task ahead but also ignited Elena's fierce determination. Each room, each artefact, each layer of dust whispered secrets of a bygone era, calling out for preservation. With her team's help, Elena was ready to breathe new life into these walls, restoring not just a building but a piece of history itself.

"We have a lot to do," Elena whispered to herself.

Although the manor was withered, she believed that there was still a way for her to fix it without changing its identity.

The air in the attic was thick with the musty, acrid scent of age and abandonment. As Elena ascended the final step, her flashlight swept across the cobweb-laden rafters, illuminating relics of the manor's storied past. Boxes stacked haphazardly and furniture draped in ghostly white sheets gave the space a forgotten, almost haunted feel. It was here, in the dim light, that Elena's beam caught the edge of an old, worn leather trunk pushed against the far wall under a sloped eave.

A whisper of caution echoed in her mind—*don't touch it. You know how this ends.* But curiosity fluttered in her chest, compelling her fingers closer to the aged leather. Some secrets were worth the risk.

As Elena stepped deeper into the attic, the temperature seemed to drop, a chill wrapping around her like an unseen cloak. A faint whisper—or was it just the wind?—brushed past her ear, sending a shiver down her spine. Her gaze locked onto the trunk nestled in the shadows, beckoning with silent insistence. She hesitated, her hand hovering over the rusted latch, as if crossing a threshold she couldn't return from. The lock was rusted, its key long lost, but with a gentle nudge from her flashlight, it gave way, revealing a trove of papers stacked neatly inside. As she lifted the first bundle of letters, tied with a faded velvet ribbon, a small cloud of dust motes danced in the beam of her light, shimmering like tiny spectres in the air.

They reminded her of the letters that she had found earlier.

Elena carefully untied the ribbon, her fingers trembling slightly with the weight of the moment. The top letter was dated 1786, written in a flowing, meticulous hand that spoke of a bygone era of inkwells and quills. The paper was brittle to the touch, and she had to handle it with utmost care to prevent it from crumbling. The letter was addressed to Miss Abigail Ashford and signed simply, "Yours ever, S."

Intrigued, Elena settled onto an old steamer trunk and began to read. The language was poetic, the words conveying a deep, fervent passion that was palpable. "My dearest Abigail," it began, "each day away from you is a torment to my soul. I count the hours until we are reunited under the starlit sky of our last embrace." The letter spoke of secret meetings, stolen moments, and a love that dared not speak its name openly. It was clear that whoever S was, his affection for Abigail was both profound and forbidden.

As Elena continued to sift through the letters, each one revealed more of the clandestine relationship. They spoke of the societal pressures of the time, the expectations placed upon Abigail by her family, and the lovers' dreams of escaping to a place where their love could flourish away from prying eyes. It was a narrative as old as time, yet each letter felt like a fresh wound of yearning and desperation.

The implications of this finding were not lost on Elena. Here, in her hands, lay not just a collection of old letters but a window into the personal lives of those who had walked the halls of the manor centuries ago. This discovery could potentially reshape the historical understanding of the manor's past and its inhabitants. The letters were a historian's treasure, offering a personal insight into the emotional landscape of the 18th century that no textbook could provide.

Her initial examination was complete; Elena gathered the letters, retying them with the velvet ribbon. Her mind was alive with questions. Who was S? How did their story end? And what could these letters reveal about the broader historical context of the era? The mystery of Abigail and her secret lover promised to be a compelling journey into the past, and Elena was determined to follow it wherever it led. A part of her told her that she should have left the letters alone, and yet the more she looked at them, the more intrigued she felt and the more she wanted to know.

Standing up, she tucked the bundle under her arm, her resolve firming. The attic, with its layers of forgotten memories, had offered up a secret that whispered of love, loss, and longing.

CHAPTER 2

The attic seemed to groan under the weight of centuries, its wooden beams stretching across the ceiling like the ribs of a forgotten beast. Elena's footsteps echoed in the vast, dust-filled space as she moved between old trunks and boxes, their surfaces long faded by time. A thick layer of dust clung to everything, stirred by her presence as if even the room resisted her intrusion.

Her mind lingered on the letter—the initial "S"—and the story it hinted at. "Yours ever, S." She couldn't shake the feeling that there was more to be found in this attic. Something deeper.

Her flashlight swept across the room, casting long shadows over cobwebbed corners and peeling wallpaper. A wooden chest in the corner, small and unassuming, caught her eye. It was different from the others—polished, well-maintained, almost as though someone had kept it safe. Forgotten but not discarded.

Elena crouched down, her fingers brushing across the brass latch. It gave with a soft click, and the chest creaked open. Inside, a stack of papers rested—sketches, their edges yellowed with age. Her breath caught. Not letters, but drawings. She lifted the first sheet carefully, tracing the lines of a bird. But underneath that—something else.

A delicate charcoal drawing lay hidden among the pages, the faint outline of a man seated with an instrument in his hands. His expression was calm, yet his posture was intense, as though every note he played carried the weight of a thousand unspoken emotions. The soft lines of his face, the relaxed but focused set of his body—it was all so intimate, so personal.

Her heart began to race as her eyes dropped to the faint script beneath the drawing. One word. Samuel.

Could it be the same Samuel from the letter? The mysterious "S" who had poured his soul out to Abigail Ashford? The thought struck her like a wave, leaving her unsteady. Samuel wasn't just a name scrawled at the bottom of a letter—he was real. Here, in her hands, was his likeness, captured by someone who had clearly known him well.

She flipped the drawing over, searching for more clues. In the bottom corner, almost faded into the paper, was another inscription: "To my muse."

Elena's breath hitched. Was this Abigail's hand? Had

she drawn this image of Samuel, the man she had loved in secret? Her mind spun with the possibilities. This wasn't just a forgotten love story—it was alive, woven into the very walls of the manor. The love between Samuel and Abigail had been real, and now, piece by piece, it was revealing itself to her.

Elena's pulse raced. Was this Samuel the same man who had written those impassioned letters to Abigail? The musician with whom she'd shared a secret, forbidden love?

Her mind raced, the pieces of the puzzle beginning to fall into place. The letter, the drawing—it was all connected. There was something hidden here, something that went far deeper than the surface story of a manor restoration. Abigail and Samuel had been real, their love had been real, and it seemed like the walls of this old house were holding onto their secrets.

Elena's fingers brushed against the brittle edge of the parchment, the faint crackle of age filling the otherwise silent room. Dust floated in the dim light, the air thick with the scent of old wood and forgotten time. She unfolded the letter carefully, afraid that any sudden movement might cause the fragile paper to crumble.

The ink was faded, but the elegant, flowing script seemed to pulse with life, pulling her into a world long past. She leaned closer, her breath catching as she began to read.

"My dearest Abigail,

Under the quiet veil of twilight, as the world about us whispers the approach of night, my thoughts turn unerringly to thee..."

The words wrapped around her like a cloak, thick with longing and whispered confessions. She could almost hear the faint strains of a melody, the ghost of a musician's hands moving across strings in the distance. Her pulse quickened, matching the rhythm of the passionate strokes of the pen. This wasn't just a letter. It was a heart bleeding out onto the page.
Her eyes skimmed further, her breath hitching.

"...how grievous this separation proves, my heart languishing in the solitude of your absence. Each hour apart stretches like the endless expanse of ocean..."

Elena shifted in her chair, her fingers tightening around the edges of the letter as the words seemed to press in on her. Samuel's voice—because that's how it felt, like his voice—echoed in her mind, each line revealing a love so raw and forbidden it stirred something deep within her.

She could picture them: Abigail, regal yet vulnerable, hiding away in some forgotten corner of the manor, her heart racing as she read Samuel's letters. And Samuel, perhaps in some dimly lit room, a single candle flickering as he penned his desires and frustrations. Their love was dangerous, each letter a secret carried through darkened hallways.

A soft sigh escaped her lips before she could stop it. She hadn't meant to get this involved. She was here to restore the manor, not lose herself in its past. But the pull of the letter, the intensity of Samuel's words... It was like staring into someone else's soul, a soul that was too similar to her own. The longing. The quiet desperation.

Her fingers trembled as she turned to the next page. The paper, fragile as it was, held more weight than she could bear at that moment. The room seemed to darken, the flicker of candlelight casting shadows that danced along the walls, as if the house itself was listening.

She swallowed hard, forcing herself to focus on the text.

"...we stand at the crossroads of passion and duty, each path fraught with loss but only one adorned with the possibility of true happiness..."

Elena's chest tightened. The letter wasn't just about love; it was a fight. A fight against the expectations of society, against the roles they'd both been forced into. She could feel Samuel's struggle in every word, the weight of what it meant to love someone he could never have.

A gust of wind rattled the window, and Elena glanced up, her heart suddenly pounding. The manor, once silent, now seemed to creak and groan around her as if it was shifting beneath her gaze. The walls, old and worn, seemed to hold their own secrets. Her fingers grazed the table, brushing aside a thin layer of dust. What else was hidden here, buried beneath centuries of neglect?

Samuel's words swirled in her mind, refusing to settle. He had hinted at something more—something beyond the love letters. Something about the manor itself. Her eyes flickered over the last lines of the letter, and her stomach dropped.

"...the manor itself holds keys to doors long thought closed, secrets that, if brought to light, could change everything..."

A chill slid down her spine, her fingers suddenly cold against the parchment. This wasn't just a story of forbidden love. It was a puzzle, a mystery hidden within the walls of the very building she'd been tasked to restore. And the pieces had been right in front of her the whole time.

She stood abruptly, the old chair scraping against the floor as she moved to the window. The air outside was still, too still, as if the world was waiting for something to happen. Elena pressed her forehead against the cool glass, staring out into the darkening sky.

She needed to know more. About Samuel. About Abigail. About whatever secrets the manor was keeping.

Her heart pounded as she turned back to the letter, fingers tracing the delicate script. Samuel and Abigail's love had been forbidden, yes, but something told her it was more than that. Something darker. More dangerous.

The walls of the manor groaned again, and she exhaled sharply. The air felt heavier now, thicker with possibility and peril.

Whatever Samuel had been trying to say, whatever Abigail had left behind, it was only the beginning. And Elena, whether she was ready or not, was caught in the middle of it all.

CHAPTER 3

Elena's fingers trembled as she leafed through the stack of letters, each piece of parchment crumbling slightly under her touch. A single candle flickered beside her, casting erratic shadows that danced along the walls as if mocking the secrets the manor held. The letters, worn and delicate, seemed to murmur their stories. The ink was faded, yet the passion within each line leapt from the page. She wanted now more than ever to uncover what lay tucked away in its depths.

As Elena sifted through the dust-covered stack of letters found in the attic, her curiosity quickly morphed into fascination. The delicate script, the faded ink, and the brittle paper transported her back in time, bridging centuries with the tender emotions captured in each line. With each letter unfolded, Elena felt a growing connection to Abigail and Samuel, whose words seemed to resonate with her own hidden desires and fears.

She couldn't entirely put her finger on it, and she felt that a part of her life was linked to theirs. She wanted their own story to have a happy ending so desperately, in a way hers never did.

She murmured lines that particularly moved her and scribbled notes in the margins of her journal, piecing together the emotional and historical landscape that shaped the lovers' lives.

If the sun were to set on our love, it would have to take me with it.

If there was ever a soul crafted from my heart, it would be yours, Abigail.

And if my melodies no longer sway you, allow my touch to relay the tunes my serenade couldn't.

Elena's eyes lingered on the flickering candlelight, the letters scattered around her like fallen leaves, each page whispering secrets of a bygone era. Her fingers traced the delicate script as if by touch, she could draw forth the defiant spirit contained within each faded line. The love between Abigail and Samuel, fierce and untamed, leapt from the pages, its raw intensity seizing Elena's heart.

The manor, once a mere restoration project, now seemed to breathe with the pulse of a forgotten era. The faded grandeur of its rooms, the hidden corners she had yet to explore—they all seemed to hum with the energy of a rebellion against the oppressive shadows of history. The stories she uncovered wove a tapestry of passion and defiance, and Elena could almost hear the echoes of their footsteps, the whispers of their secret rendezvous in the creaking corridors.

As she read the final letter, her resolve solidified. The manor was no longer just a building to be restored; it was a vessel carrying the weight of lost voices and untold stories. She imagined the laughter and longing that once filled its halls, their love lingering like the scent of a distant perfume. Each word from the past ignited a fire within her, pushing her beyond the boundaries of professional duty into a realm of personal commitment.

Standing amidst the scattered letters, Elena felt a fierce determination swell within her. She would delve deeper, unearth every hidden chamber, and bring Abigail and Samuel's story to light. The manor's secrets, once veiled in shadow, would be uncovered and celebrated. She would not rest until their love was fully revealed, its brilliance shining through the annals of time.

The content of Abigail and Samuel's letters provided a vivid window into the formidable societal pressures and family expectations that framed their secret romance. These letters, penned with a mix of defiance and despair, unveiled the couple's acute awareness of the barriers erected by their 18th-century British society.

It showed how easily two people could live in the same world, and yet they would be able to live two completely different lives. Yet even then, one chance encounter could bring both of them together.

His letters also touched on the personal sacrifices he had made to pursue his love for Abigail, from his secrecy to the risk of social ostracism and professional ruin. He had found his pearl in a sea of stones, and he wasn't about to let go of her.

The lovers' correspondence often delved into their clandestine meetings, which they described as moments of blissful escape from the oppressive norms that governed their public lives. After their first encounter, Abigail and Samuel took any chance to meet each other. Abigail found herself sneaking out of her bedroom window multiple times a week. The letters detailed their strategies to avoid suspicion and the coded messages they use to communicate, painting a picture of a couple fighting to preserve their bond against overwhelming odds. Abigail would often confide in her sister Mary about Samuel as she was the only person she knew that she could trust and she knew would always have her back. The more she read through the narratives, the more Elena gained insights into the wit and courage required for their romance to survive in an era where such liaisons could lead not only to social death but also to real peril.

These letters did more than just chronicle a forbidden love; they served as a testament to the human spirit's capacity for resilience. As Elena pored over these missives, her admiration for the couple deepened, and she felt a profound connection to their plight, which mirrored the challenges she faced in her own life.

After she had lost her family, Elena had wanted to give up, and she had done so multiple times. It had taken a lot inside of her not to give up on her strife, and she had dug her feet deep into the rich history of her country in order to avoid falling into her own debilitating thoughts. However, Abigail and Samuel's story reminded her of the reason why she did all of this in the first place. She knew every story deserved to be heard, and she was intent on making sure they were.

The struggles of Abigail and Samuel inspired Elena to view the manor not just as a structure of wood and stone but as a bastion of historical truths waiting to be told. Through their story, she was reminded of the power of love to challenge the status quo and the importance of telling such stories to ensure they are not lost to the annals of time.

As Elena continued her exploration of the letters, her attention was drawn to a series of cryptic mentions and allusions that suggested the existence of further secrets ensconced within the manor's aged walls.

"The manor has become a refuge for the both of us. And even when you are not here, Abigail, I find myself replaying our shared moments and longing for your return. Each room we have made our own has become

ingrained in my existence, and although our love remains hidden much like the rooms. I know one day they will be brought to light."

"Late at night, I find myself reminiscing about those brief moments we shared in the shadowed corners. Wishing that I could make them last a little longer. That you, my dear Samuel, could be someone I present to my father in defiance. However, I know now isn't the time, but I hold onto the hope that our time will indeed come soon."

As she meticulously examined the letters, Elena noticed recurring references to "the guardian's nook", "the watchtower", and "the shadowed corner", phrases that Abigail used in her letters to describe secret meeting spots within the manor.

Intrigued, Elena decided to cross-reference these mentions with the manor's blueprints and discovered inconsistencies that suggested modifications were made to the building's structure that are not documented in any public records. This revelation points to possible hidden rooms or compartments that may have served as safe havens for lovers or as hiding spots for their correspondence or other forbidden items.

Now this is interesting.

Elena's scrutiny also revealed several letters with pressed flowers and leaves. The flowers appeared to be purple lilacs. A rarity in that region, however, they seemed to peak her excitement. As she had expected when she examined the journal documenting the gardens, she identified the plants as species native to a secluded part of the manor's grounds. The journal documented the location of the garden, mapping it with tall, secluded trees and a long wooden bench under the shade of the oak tree.

As the night deepened, Elena's resolve pulled her into the cold embrace of the manor's garden. The moonlight cast a ghostly glow over the overgrown grounds, the once-pristine hedges now tangled in shadows. Each step she took crunched against a blanket of dried leaves, their brittle sound echoing through the eerie silence. The air, crisp and tinged with the faint scent of decay, seemed to carry whispers of long-forgotten secrets.

The garden, veiled in a shroud of darkness, appeared as a spectral remnant of its former self. Weeds sprawled unchecked, clawing at the worn wooden bench that stood like a forgotten sentinel amidst the encroaching wildness. Elena's breath formed fleeting clouds in the chill, each exhale mingling with the mist that curled around her feet.

As she ventured deeper, her flashlight's beam trembled, casting wavering shadows that danced menacingly among the twisted branches. Her eyes fell upon the old oak, its gnarled bark etched with carvings that seemed to pulse with a faint, almost supernatural luminescence. The initials "A" and "S" intertwined in the cold, ancient wood, their presence a haunting testament to the love that had once flourished in this forsaken corner.

Elena's pulse quickened as she traced the initials with trembling fingers, the chill of the night air seeping through her gloves. The garden, with its spectral beauty and lingering echoes of the past, seemed to whisper of the secrets it had long kept hidden.

A bright grin made its way onto her features at the sight. This was the first sign that she had gotten that Abigail and Samuel were real people who had lived actual lives within the walls of the manor. That pushed her to go back to the journals and find more and learn more.

As Elena pieced together these clues, her vision of the manor as a mere restoration project broadens into a quest to unearth a hidden narrative of resistance and defiance. Each discovery fuelled her determination to bring to light not just the story of a forbidden romance but a chapter of history that reflects the struggles and aspirations of those who dared to defy their society.

Each letter held a new clue and added layers to the historical tapestry she was weaving, making the manor not just a site of architectural interest but a portal to a turbulent and passionate past.

As Elena sifted through the last of the faded letters, her initial intrigue transformed into a profound commitment. Each word from the past had drawn her deeper into the enigmatic history of the manor and the lives of Abigail and Samuel. Her role as a restorer began to blur with that of a detective and historian, driven to uncover the truth hidden within these walls.

The emotional weight of the letters—each confession and secret rendezvous detailed on the worn paper—stirs a resonant connection within Elena. She realises that these aren't just remnants of a bygone romance but a mosaic of stories and secrets that could offer new insights into the social fabric of the 18th century. Her academic curiosity, combined with a growing personal attachment to the story, fuels her resolve to give voice to those who lived their truths in the shadows of history.

CHAPTER 4

Thomas Reynolds stepped into the manor, his boots echoing softly on the worn stone floor of the entrance hall. The air within was thick and musty, clinging to the skin like the weight of time itself. The walls, once stately, now sagged under the pressure of neglect, streaked with damp where ivy tendrils had forced their way through cracks in the stone. His gaze followed the lines of decay, noting every flaw with a practised eye while the distant sounds of footsteps and muted voices reverberated through the empty corridors.

He had seen worse. But something about this place stirred unease in him, a sense that the manor resisted change, clinging to its secrets with a tenacity that was almost palpable. As he moved deeper into the foyer, his fingers brushed against the cold iron of an ornate bannister, and he winced at the faint tremor beneath his touch. The structure was unsound.

"Mr. Reynolds, I presume?"

The voice startled him from his thoughts, a blend of professionalism and warmth but with an edge that cut through the gloom. He turned, his eyes meeting those of a woman striding toward him with confident steps. Her silhouette was framed by the dim light spilling through a large, dust-covered window, casting her features into partial shadow. Her dark brown hair pulled back, contrasted with the soft curve of her cheek, and her suit was fitted tightly to her slender form, emphasising her movements with a graceful precision. Yet there was something about her —the sharpness of her gaze, perhaps—that unsettled him.

"I'm Elena Reynolds," she continued, offering her hand. "I'm overseeing the restoration."

Thomas hesitated, taking her hand firmly, his expression neutral. "Good to meet you, Miss Reynolds. I see you've wasted no time." His tone was clipped, though he allowed a faint smile to soften it. Her work ethic had preceded her, but he was cautious, especially when it came to those who let sentimentality interfere with preservation.

Elena's smile faltered, a faint blush colouring her cheeks as she withdrew her hand. "I couldn't resist. The manor has a way of drawing you in."

Thomas grunted, casting a glance at the peeling tarmac and sagging beams. "It draws you in, alright, but not in the way you'd hope. This place is crumbling beneath the surface."

The silence stretched between them, weighted by the heavy air and the moaning of wind through the broken windows. Thomas moved deeper into the room, his fingers grazing the cracked walls, eyes narrowed as he assessed the damage. He crouched by the skirting, his hand brushing away a layer of dust to reveal deep fissures in the stonework.

"This is worse than I expected." He stood and gestured toward the crack that ran the length of the wall. "We'll be lucky if the foundation holds another winter."

Elena followed his gaze, her lips tightening. She wrapped her arms around herself unconsciously, as if the chill in the room had finally settled into her bones. "I was hoping we could salvage more of the original structure," she said softly.

"You can hope," Thomas replied, his voice matter of fact. "But it won't save these walls. They're too far gone. We need to reinforce the entire foundation, or this place will collapse within the year." His words were blunt, and though Elena's face remained calm, he caught the slight tremor in her breath.

"I'll show you the basement," she said, her voice betraying none of her frustration. "That's where the real trouble lies."

They descended the narrow, winding staircase in silence, the steps creaking beneath their weight. The air grew cooler and damper with each step, carrying with it the scent of decay and wet stone. Water pooled at the edges of the uneven floor, and the walls were slick with mildew. Thomas' breath caught in his throat. This was more than neglect—this was rot.

"We'll need to pump the water out, seal the leaks, and reinforce the walls before we can even think about restoring anything above ground," he murmured, the low timbre of his voice echoing through the dimly lit basement. "This is going to take time—more than I think you've planned for."

Elena nodded, but there was a tension in her posture now, a rigidity that belied her calm demeanour. "I understand," she said, though her tone was clipped. "But the manor's history is important, too. We can't just tear it apart to make way for the new."

Thomas glanced at her sideways. "History doesn't mean much if there's no building left to tell it." His eyes scanned the ceiling, the thick cobwebs swaying gently in the damp breeze. "If we don't stabilise this place, you'll have nothing but a ruin. Is that what you want?"

Her gaze hardened, the light in her eyes turning cold. "Of course not. But I believe we can do both—restore the manor and preserve its integrity. You might be concerned with the bones of this place, but I'm concerned with its soul."

Thomas said nothing at first, but his fingers clenched around the clipboard he carried, the paper crinkling under his grip. He had dealt with sentimentality before, but this—this was something else. He straightened, fixing her with a steady gaze.

"Then we'll need to make compromises," he said slowly, measuring his words. "Otherwise, this whole project will fall apart. You need to be willing to let go of some things."

Her jaw tightened, but she held his gaze. "And you need to remember that this manor is more than just wood and stone. It's a piece of history, and we owe it to those who lived here to respect that."

The tension between them crackled like the distant sound of thunder, heavy and unspoken. Thomas could feel the weight of the conversation lingering, pressing against the walls of the old manor like the years of neglect that had settled there. He respected her conviction, but it was clear that they were standing at opposite ends of a battlefield they hadn't yet fully entered.

As they ascended the staircase, the creaks and groans beneath their feet seemed louder, as if the manor itself were listening, waiting for the resolution of the conflict brewing between them. Neither spoke until they reached the top, and even then, the silence stretched, taut and uneasy.

Elena led Thomas to the drawing room, where the rest of the restoration team awaited. The room itself seemed to hum with the past, dust swirling through the shafts of light streaming in from the tall, arched windows. The air smelled faintly of old wood and mildew, a reminder of the building's fragility. Each creak of the floor beneath their feet seemed to echo longer than it should have, as if the manor itself was groaning under the weight of centuries.

The team sat around a large oak table, scattered with blueprints, sketches, and old photographs. Sophie, with her curly hair falling over her face, was the first to break the silence. She beamed at Thomas, rising to her feet and extending her hand in an overly enthusiastic welcome.

"Welcome to the team, Mr. Reynolds! We're so excited to have you here. It feels like we're assembling the Avengers or something!" Her words were met with a soft chuckle from Aarav and a tired sigh from Clara.

Thomas, however, didn't seem amused. He gave her a curt nod and shook her hand, his eyes scanning the room with a calculating gaze. "It's a pleasure. Let's hope we can save this place before it falls apart completely."

Sophie, undeterred by his lack of enthusiasm, nodded eagerly. "Oh, don't worry! We've got spirit, and that counts for something, right?"

"Spirit doesn't hold walls up," Thomas replied, the corners of his mouth twitching, almost but not quite forming a smile.

Elena watched the exchange with a slight smile, though her eyes flickered with the same discomfort she had felt earlier. She cleared her throat to regain control of the room. "Thomas, meet the rest of the team. Sophie is our historian. Aarav, our structural engineer, and Clara, our project manager."

Aarav adjusted his glasses, stepping forward. "So, Thomas, what's your initial impression of the place? Think we can pull this off?"

Thomas took a moment, his gaze lingering on the deep cracks snaking up the walls. "The structure has potential, but the decay runs deep. I'm concerned about the integrity of the foundation and the water damage in the lower levels. Some walls will need to come down. We can salvage what we can, but I won't promise miracles."

There was a pause. The air felt tense, weighted with unspoken concerns. Elena, sensing the unease among her team, stepped in, her tone light but firm. "We are here to restore the manor, not tear it down, remember?"

Thomas turned to her, his expression unreadable. "We're here to ensure it stands for another hundred years. That means making some sacrifices."

Sophie's bright smile faltered. "But we can't replace everything, can we? Isn't the whole point to preserve as much as we can?"

"That's the ideal, yes," Thomas said, his tone steady but firm. "But ideals don't keep a roof from caving in. Safety has to come first. Sentiment is a luxury we can't afford."

Elena's jaw tightened, though she kept her voice measured. "We understand the importance of safety, Thomas. But history isn't something you can just replace with steel beams and concrete. We have to find a balance."

Before Thomas could respond, Aarav chimed in. "Thomas, you'll like our plan for the foundation. We've identified the weakest points, and I think we can reinforce them without losing too much of the original stonework."

Thomas nodded, flipping through the pages on his clipboard. "I'll take a look. But don't be too attached to anything yet. If it's beyond saving, it goes."

Clara, who had been quiet until now, finally spoke up. Her voice was calm but carried an edge. "We've got a timeline to meet and a budget that's already tight. We can't afford to waste time debating every brick and beam."

"Agreed," Thomas said, his eyes locking with Elena's for a brief moment. "We'll see what's worth saving. But no promises."

The conversation lulled for a beat, the atmosphere thick with an undercurrent of tension. Thomas, despite his rigid demeanour, couldn't help but sense the camaraderie among the team—a warmth he hadn't felt in his previous projects. They were passionate, perhaps too passionate for his liking, but there was a fire in their determination that reminded him of something long buried within himself.

Elena's gaze lingered on Thomas, studying him. He was a man of calculation and structure, but beneath his hard exterior, there was something else. Something she couldn't quite place yet.

"Well," she said, breaking the silence, "I guess we'll have to see whose vision prevails." There was a challenge in her voice, though softened by a small smile.

Thomas tilted his head slightly, considering her. "I guess we will."

CHAPTER 5

In the dimly lit corner of the music room, where dust motes danced in the slanting light, Elena carefully unfolded the aged parchment she had discovered tucked behind an ancient piano.

She had come into the room in the hopes of spending some time away from the bustling chaos going on outside. She was shocked to find the grand piano. It was etched with intricate markings and letters etched on its side. A smile came over her features as she remembered her grandmother, who had a thing for musical instruments. She used to sit Elena on her lap every Saturday afternoon as they listened to the orchestra on the radio. They would always share dreams of going to a play when Elena was older. Unfortunately, her grandmother died before that was possible.

As she smoothed out the creases, the ink, faded but still legible, seemed to pulse with the life of its long-ago author, Abigail. The letter, addressed to Samuel, was a window into a hidden past, written with a passion that transcended the centuries.

Abigail's words were crafted with a careful blend of caution and yearning, her script flowing elegantly across the page. "My dearest Samuel," the letter began, "each moment away from you is an eternity of torment, yet I am bound by the constraints of my station and the watchful eyes that govern my every move. These few fleeting moments we have shared in this manor are my free moments of solace and the piano room, where we had shared our first kiss; my sanctuary of bliss…" Here, Abigail laid bare the excruciating duality of her situation—caught between her societal obligations and her undying affection for a man deemed unsuitable by her family.

The music room, she detailed, was their haven, the only place where the strictures of 18th-century society temporarily dissolved. Here, they were perfectly alone, in a place where their love could blossom freely, without fear of interruption or being seen. *"Within these walls, beneath the harmonies of our clandestine sonatas, I find a semblance of freedom. The notes you play resonate not just in the air but within the very fabric of my being, each chord a declaration of our forbidden love."* Her descriptions painted a vivid picture of their meetings: the careful timing of their encounters, the way the music masked their whispers, and how the room, with its heavy curtains and sound-swelling acoustics, kept their secrets.

Elena, feeling a surge of connection to Abigail, imagined the young woman waiting anxiously for the cover of night, the only time the manor's strict surveillance relaxed enough for Samuel to slip through the servants' entrance. The danger of their meetings was palpable in Abigail's recounting, with every stolen moment shadowed by the risk of discovery. "*We are but shadows in this grand tapestry of propriety,*" Abigail wrote, "*moving silent and unseen, yet fiercely alive in our quiet rebellion.*"

The letter also hinted at the depth of their emotional intimacy, showing how the music room became a metaphor for their relationship—hidden yet vibrant, constrained yet expressive. Abigail's prose was interspersed with musical notations, a secret code of sorts that illustrated the tunes Samuel would play for her, each one symbolising different facets of their journey together. These snippets of melody woven into her words suggested that music was their language of love, understood only by them.

As Elena read on, the weight of the lovers' predicament became even clearer. Abigail's final paragraphs were a mix of hope and despair, a poignant acknowledgement of the likelihood that their love might be doomed, yet tempered by the resolve to cherish each fleeting moment. "Though we may never walk in daylight together, in the twilight of our music room, we are free. Here, I am yours, and you are mine, in defiance of the world outside."

Closing the letter, Elena felt a profound respect for the

young lovers' bravery and a renewed determination to uncover the full story of their hidden romance. The music room, a silent witness to their love, awaited her exploration, promising more secrets held within its walls. The task ahead was clear: to piece together the fragments of this historical love affair and restore the voices that time had nearly silenced.

As Elena carefully re-folded the letter, placing it beside her notes, her mind buzzed with the implications of what she'd just read. She looked around the music room, now silent and empty, the echoes of the past somehow louder in the stillness. The room, with its high ceilings and grand piano, no longer felt just like a part of the manor's restoration project; it was a portal into Abigail and Samuel's world.

The weight of responsibility to tell their story truthfully weighed on her, mingling with an excitement that only a historian feels when on the cusp of a significant discovery. It was clear to Elena that the music room was more than a setting for clandestine meetings; it was a symbol of the couple's resilience and creativity in the face of societal constraints.

Eager to understand more about the physical space where the lovers had shared so many moments, Elena decided to examine the room more closely. She walked over to the piano, the one mentioned in Abigail's letters, its wood dull and worn by time but still majestic. Running her fingers over the keys, she could almost hear the faint strains of the music Samuel had played for Abigail, each note a defiance of the rigid societal norms they were bound by.

Opening the piano's lid, Elena was not surprised to find it well-maintained. She knew from the letters that Samuel, though of humble origin, was a skilled musician, likely having taken great care of his only solace and voice. As she pressed a key, the sound was surprisingly clear, a testament to the quality of the instrument and the care it had received over the centuries.

Turning her attention from the piano, Elena began to inspect the walls and floorboards, searching for any hidden compartments or clues that might have been overlooked in the past. Her thoroughness paid off when she noticed a slight discrepancy in the wall panelling behind the piano. With a mix of anticipation and care, she prodded at the area, and to her delight, a hidden drawer slid open.

Inside, she found a small, leather-bound journal, its pages yellowed but preserved. The cover bore no name, but Elena felt a surge of triumph—this could only belong to Samuel or Abigail. She carefully opened it, finding entries in a hand that matched the letters, confirming it was indeed Abigail's. The journal entries provided a more personal, day-to-day account of her thoughts and emotions during the time of her secret romance with Samuel.

Each entry was a piece of the puzzle, providing insight into the hardships and joys they experienced. Abigail wrote about the societal expectations placed upon her as an aristocrat, her fear of the consequences they would face if discovered, and her dreams of a life free from the chains of her lineage.

"To be a woman in this world is to be propped up like a trophy for only the highest victor to attain. I find it draining that I constantly have to perform and display myself like some type of award in order to feel seen and heard. And yet, even then, only he truly sees me."

Elena knew this journal was a treasure trove of information that could bring depth to the story she aimed to tell. As she continued reading, she felt a profound connection to Abigail, a woman who had lived centuries ago but whose feelings and desires resonated across time. This connection reaffirmed Elena's resolve to bring the story of Abigail and Samuel to light, not just as a tale of forbidden love but as a testament to the enduring power of human emotion and connection.

"Before Samuel, my life had been consumed by nothingness, and if my father finds a husband for me, a day comes when I will have to leave him. I know that it is nothingness I will return to."

As the shadows lengthened in the music room, Elena sat, enveloped in the past, ready to dive deeper into the lives of two people who had turned this room into their sanctuary. With the journal in hand and the letters as her guide, she was ready to reconstruct a forgotten chapter of history, ensuring that the voices of Abigail and Samuel were heard once more.

"Every day with you feels like a soft symphony echoing against my heart and a new tune being crafted."

In the grand scheme of the manor's sprawling architecture, the music room held a discreet charm that seemed to whisper secrets of ages past. This room, with its ornate mouldings and large, arched windows, offered a panoramic view of the verdant gardens, now overgrown with the wildness of neglect. The soft, filtered light through the stained glass painted colourful patterns on the floor, adding a touch of surreal beauty to the space that had witnessed countless clandestine meetings between Abigail and Samuel.

The music room was more than just a backdrop to their romance; it was their sanctuary, a place where the social barriers of the outside world could momentarily dissolve through the harmony of Samuel's music.

The piano, a magnificent piece crafted from mahogany, stood proudly as the centrepiece of the room. Its keys, though silent now, once echoed melodies that carried the weight of unsaid words and unexpressed feelings. It was here that Samuel expressed his love for Abigail through compositions that were as complex and profound as their feelings for each other. Each piece he played was a testament to their love, a defiance of the rigid norms that sought to keep them apart.

For Elena, the discovery of the diary in this music room was a transformative experience. The room, with each of its carefully crafted details, from the faded tapestries to the chandelier that hung from the ceiling like a silent witness to the past, brought a palpable sense of immediacy and urgency to the love story.

This emotional impact deepened Elena's connection to Abigail and Samuel. She felt a kinship with Abigail, a woman who had dared to love beyond the constraints of her circumstances, and a respect for Samuel, who had risked everything for the chance at a life with the woman he loved. The music room, with its blend of beauty and secrecy, symbolised their struggle and their passion, making it an essential piece of the puzzle that Elena was determined to solve.

Elena's hands trembled slightly as she held the diary, its leather cover worn with age. As she carefully closed it, a page slipped out and fluttered to the floor. She hurriedly retrieved it, her heart pounding as she unfolded the note. The writing was unmistakably Samuel's, elegant and filled with urgency:

"Let's run away. Let's go to France. Meet me under our tree this May 21st when the sun sets. Here are two tickets for the Bella boat."

Elena's breath caught in her throat. She glanced back at the diary, noticing the space where the tickets should have been. The absence of the tickets was a striking omission, a piece of the puzzle that seemed to tell its own story.

Her mind raced with the implications. The note was a clear invitation to escape, to leave behind their constrained lives for a new beginning in France. The fact that the tickets were no longer there suggested that Abigail and Samuel might have followed through on their plan—perhaps they had eloped, seizing their chance at freedom despite the obstacles.

Elena carefully folded the note and placed it back into the diary, her resolve solidifying with each movement. "We need to make their story the centrepiece of the exhibition. It's more than just a historical detail—it's a testament to their courage and their love."

Understanding the significance of the music room not only in the context of Abigail and Samuel's relationship but also in the broader narrative of the manor's history became a driving force for Elena. She realised that this room could serve as a key exhibit in the eventual restoration and public presentation of the manor. By highlighting the room and its role in their story, she could bring an authentic and touching element to the historical retelling, making the manor not just a place of historical interest, but a beacon of human emotion and artistic expression.

Her plan included meticulous restoration of the room's original features—repairing the intricate parquet floors, restoring the faded wall frescoes, and tuning the old piano to concert standard. Each element was considered not only for its aesthetic value but also for its ability to convey the story of Abigail and Samuel. The restored piano would not be just a display piece; it would be played during guided tours, its music filling the room as it might have centuries ago, providing a sensory experience that connected visitors directly to the room's historical romance.

She was determined to keep the original keys and strings of the piano. Although the wood was partially chipped, with much effort, she was able to polish it up and made sure that it didn't crack any further. The white tiles that lay on the base of the wall had small black and white piano tiles on them, and although she couldn't keep all of them, she decided to keep a single row. The rest of the walls were made of refurbished wood panels.

Elena also thought about utilising modern technology to enhance the historical ambience. She had begun to understand the point Thomas was trying to make. It wasn't just about bringing the past stories to life. It was also about preserving the current state of the manor. Subtle, ambient soundtracks could simulate the kind of music Samuel might have composed, played softly in the background. At the same time, augmented reality features could allow visitors to see the room as it would have appeared in Abigail's time. Through these layers of restoration and innovation, the music room would serve as a bridge between the past and the present, making the historical experiences palpable for contemporary audiences.

As she detailed her ideas in the project proposal, Elena felt a profound connection to her work, spurred by the discovery of the letters. Her approach went beyond simple preservation; she aimed to revive the manor's soul, with the music room as its beating heart. This endeavour, she believed, would not only honour the memory of the manor's historical occupants, but also rekindle the essence of their experiences for others to feel and appreciate.

CHAPTER 6

Elena's examination of the piano was thorough. She inspected each carved nook and hidden cranny, her flashlight revealing secrets held within its aged wood. Inside the body of the piano, beneath the lifted lid, she discovered initials carved into the wood—'A.S.'—a tangible testament to Abigail and Samuel's secret rendezvous.

The exploration continued with meticulous care. Elena photographed every angle of the piano, recorded anomalies, and sketched the layout of the room. She hypothesised that the lovers might have utilised this space: perhaps the piano served as a shield from prying eyes, and its music was a cover for whispered words of love. She imagined Abigail and Samuel sitting side by side on the piano stool, Samuel playing a melody while they dreamed of a future together.

Through her detailed investigation, Elena not only

documented the physical space but also stepped into the emotional echoes of the past. Touching the keys that Samuel once played and standing in the quiet solitude of the room, she felt a profound connection to their story. Her investigation became a personal journey into the essence of the music room—a narrative woven from love, secrecy, and timeless melodies.

Elena paced back and forth in the music room, her fingers trailing lightly over the dusty surface of the grand piano. The sunlight filtering through the tall windows cast soft patterns on the floor, accentuating the room's faded elegance. She had been grappling with her feelings for days—both the weight of Abigail and Samuel's story and her growing frustration with Thomas's scepticism.

Taking a deep breath, she decided it was time to confront the bane of her existence. She glanced at Thomas, who was examining the main living room with a critical eye.

"Thomas, there's something I need to share with you," she said, her voice tinged with both excitement and apprehension.

He looked up, eyebrows raised in curiosity. "What's up?"

"I found something in the attic—some old letters," Elena began, her fingers nervously fiddling with the edge of a piece of parchment she'd brought along. "They're from the 18th century."

Thomas's expression shifted from curiosity to concern. "The attic? You went up there? That place is a death trap."

Elena gave a small, self-deprecating laugh. "Yes, I know it's a mess. But I couldn't resist. These letters... they're between two people named Abigail and Samuel. It's a whole love story."

Thomas's eyes widened. "A love story? Amazing, two people loved each other two hundred years ago. Get over it, Elena. We have work to do here".

Elena immediately felt rage inside her. However, she decided to stay calm.

"The letters describe their secret meetings, their hopes, their fears. It's like stepping into their world. And... they're so much more than just old paper. They also speak about the manor and hidden rooms."

Thomas's worry shifted to interest. "Show me. I need to see these letters."

Elena handed him the letters, watching as he carefully unfolded one.

"I wasn't sure if I should tell you right away. I know you're busy, and I didn't want to distract you."

Thomas glanced up, a smile tugging at the corner of his mouth.

"Distract me? This is the best kind of distraction. Besides, it seems like you've found something that might actually justify all this renovation fuss."

Elena chuckled, her nerves easing slightly. "I think it's more than just a distraction. These letters might be the key to understanding more about the history of this manor. I've also found Abigail's diary. There was a note from Samuel; they were planning to escape to France, and the boat tickets were nowhere to be found."

Thomas studied the letters, his earlier scepticism melting away as he read. "Alright, Elena. Let's see where this love story leads us. But next time, maybe don't risk life and limb for old papers."

Elena laughed softly, her relief palpable. "Deal. Thank you. I knew you'd appreciate the find."

Thomas grinned, his eyes meeting hers with a newfound respect.

"I need to show you something else," added Elena before leaving, an eye over her shoulder to be sure that Thomas was following. She tried to steady her nerves, her emotions a turbulent sea beneath her calm exterior.

Elena stood at the threshold of the music room, her heart heavy with the weight of the piano's history. It was not just any restoration; it was a connection to a love story long forgotten. Thomas, still wrapped up in his practical approach to the manor's restoration, was standing beside her, eyeing the grand piano with a mix of scepticism and curiosity.

"Thomas, I need to talk to you about something,"

Elena began, her voice wavering slightly. She tried to steady her nerves, her emotions a turbulent sea beneath her calm exterior.

Thomas glanced over, raising an eyebrow. "Alright, Elena. What's up? If you're going to tell me the piano's secretly an ancient artefact, I might need a drink first."

Elena rolled her eyes, a half-smile tugging at her lips. "Well, if you're not too busy being a professional sceptic, I'd appreciate your expertise."

Thomas raised an eyebrow. "Professional sceptic, huh? And what's that? Someone who questions everything, even the obvious?"

"Pretty much," Elena said, her smile widening. "But here's the thing—I need you to help me with the piano."

Thomas's expression softened slightly. "Alright, you've got my attention. What's the big deal?"

Elena took a deep breath, her hands gripping the edges of her notes. "You know those letters I found? Abigail's letters? They describe this piano in detail—how it was a secret haven for her and Samuel. There's a whole backstory about their hidden meetings and their love. It's... it's really emotional."

Thomas's scepticism flickered but remained intact. "Okay, so it's a sentimental relic. What's the real issue?"

Elena's eyes sparkled with a mix of frustration and affection. "The issue is that this piano is more than just wood and keys. It's a tangible link to their story. They carved their initials into it, for heaven's sake! I found 'A.S.' inside the lid. I found sketches that Abigail made—sketches of the manor of Samuel. This isn't just about restoring an old instrument; it's about honouring their story."

Thomas studied her, his gaze softening. "You're passionate about this."

Elena nodded, her voice trembling slightly. "Yes, and I need your help. I know we don't always see eye to eye, but... I believe that if we work together, we can restore this piano properly and preserve the essence of their story."

Thomas tilted his head, a grin spreading across his face. "You know, Elena, you're kind of like a walking historical romance novel. Just with fewer swooning heroines and more dust."

Elena laughed, a genuine, heartfelt sound. "I suppose I am. And you're the grumpy editor who needs convincing. So, what do you say? Will you help me bring this piano—and its story—back to life?"

Thomas sighed dramatically, but his eyes were warm. "Alright, alright. I'll help. But only if you promise to stop making me sound like the villain in your melodramas."

Elena's smile was radiant. "Deal. And who knows? You might even enjoy this. I hear historical romance novels are making a comeback."

Thomas chuckled, shaking his head. "I'll stick to the restoration work, thank you very much. But if it means I get to see you this passionate, I might even read one of those novels."

Elena's eyes sparkled with mischief. "Just wait until you see the rest of the findings. We might even have to rename the room 'Abigail and Samuel's Love Nest.'"

Thomas laughed, the sound echoing through the music room. "You're impossible, Elena. But alright, let's get to work. The sooner we restore this piano, the sooner we can get back to more normal restoration tasks—like fixing the roof or battling with the squirrels in the attic."

Elena grinned, her heart lighter. "Agreed. But let's enjoy this while we can. After all, how often do we get to be part of a love story?"

Thomas gave her a playful salute. "To historical romance and secret love stories, then. Lead the way, and I'll follow."

As they worked side by side, the tension between them eased, replaced by a shared sense of purpose and camaraderie. The music room, with its restored piano and renewed energy, became a testament not only to the past but to their evolving partnership.

CHAPTER 7

Elena stood in the attic, the low light casting long shadows across the aged floorboards. The air was thick with the scent of dust and time, and every creak underfoot felt like the weight of history pressing down. She brushed a cobweb from her shoulder and eyed the stack of old crates ahead. She had survived the attic once already—barely—but something in her gut told her that this time, she wouldn't leave without unearthing something significant.

Thomas stepped in behind her, his boots muffled by the dust-covered floor. "Well, you were right. This place is a maze of forgotten things," he remarked, his voice low as if not to disturb the silence.

She smiled faintly, not looking back at him. "I've survived this attic once already, you know. I think I can handle a few more layers of dust."

He chuckled softly, bending to examine a crate. "Just

making sure you don't disappear into the shadows this time."

As they worked through the clutter, the dim light of the attic illuminated an old wooden box, weathered with age but still intact. Elena's fingers traced the carvings on the lid, intricate and faded. She carefully lifted the latch, her breath catching when she uncovered its contents: faded letters, a few yellowed photographs, and something that looked like a diary.

"These must be from the early 1800s," Thomas mused as he knelt beside her, picking up one of the photographs. He turned it over gently in his hands. "Look at the sepia tones, how the edges have curled... They've aged remarkably." His voice was soft, reverent almost.

Elena felt a pang in her chest, a weight settling in her stomach as she sifted through the letters. Each one was a relic of the past, a snapshot of lives long gone, but the names written in the spidery handwriting felt all too familiar. Abigail. Samuel. She could almost feel their presence in the room, their secrets whispering through the still air.

"Elena," Thomas's voice brought her back, "these letters... They're from Abigail and Samuel, aren't they?"

She nodded, unable to form words for a moment. "It's their story," she finally whispered. "A forbidden love. The kind that gets buried with the dead and forgotten. But not entirely." She met his eyes, and for a brief second, the weight of the manor's history hung between them.

Thomas raised an eyebrow. "I thought you didn't believe in ghost stories."

She managed a small, tight-lipped smile. "Maybe I'm starting to change my mind."

There was a pause, a quiet moment where the past seemed to weave into the present. Elena let herself linger on the words in the letters, trying to imagine the fear and passion behind every stroke of the pen. They had risked everything—reputation, family, their future—for something they knew could never be. And here she was, unearthing it all.

Thomas broke the silence, glancing toward the others downstairs. "You should show the team this. It's not just about restoring the manor anymore. This is a piece of its soul."

Elena inhaled deeply, the weight of his words settling over her. She rose to her feet, gathering the letters and photos, feeling the significance of what they had found pulse through her. "Let's go," she said, her voice steady though her heart raced.

As they descended back into the manor's more familiar halls, the distant murmur of conversation and the clink of glasses grew louder. The restoration team was gathered in the drawing room, their laughter carrying through the air, oblivious to the gravity of what Elena had just discovered.

The moment she stepped into the room, eyes turned to her.

Elena exchanged a glance with Thomas, feeling a strange mix of excitement and apprehension. "You'll want to see this."

She took a deep breath, glancing at Thomas for a brief second before continuing.

"In the attic and earlier in the music room, I discovered letters... dozens of them. Hidden away, as if someone didn't want them to be found." Her voice softened as she added, "They tell the story of Abigail Ashford, one of the manor's original inhabitants, and her forbidden relationship with a man named Samuel. He was a musician who lived nearby."

The team stilled, their curiosity piqued, but a tension hung in the air. Sophie was the first to break it. "A forbidden relationship? Why wasn't it allowed?"

Elena nodded, her expression darkening with the weight of the truth.

"Abigail came from a wealthy, prestigious family—one with influence and a name to uphold. Samuel, though..." She paused, glancing down at the worn letters in her hands, feeling the fragility of their story. "Samuel was a commoner. Her family never would have accepted him. They wrote to each other in secret, met here in the manor's music room, and planned to run away together."

"But something went wrong," she added, her voice quieter now. "Something we still don't understand. The letters end abruptly. There are hints of something tragic, something that tore them apart, but we haven't pieced it together yet."

A murmur ran through the group as they absorbed this revelation. Clara leaned back in her chair, arching an eyebrow.

"So, a tragic love story buried in the walls of this place?" She cast a quick glance at Thomas. "And you two have been working on this together?"

Elena ignored Clara's insinuation, keeping her focus on the letters. "It's more than just a story. There's a real history here, one that's been forgotten—deliberately hidden, even. These letters... they're intimate, raw. Abigail and Samuel risked everything to be together, but we don't know what happened in the end." She paused, the mystery still gnawing at her.

"We don't know if they ever got a chance to run. Or if someone stopped them."

Thomas shifted beside her, glancing at the rest of the team. "She's been sharing this with me over the past few days," he added, carefully choosing his words.

Clara, who had been quiet, couldn't help but snort. "You've been sharing it with *him*? The guy you supposedly can't stand?" Her eyes gleamed with a mischievous edge as she tilted her head toward Elena. "Seems like you two have your own little secret, don't you?"

Elena felt a flush of heat rush to her cheeks, but she quickly masked it with a shrug. "He's just the most qualified to help me piece it all together," she replied casually, though the weight of Clara's comment lingered.

"Right," Clara said, her voice dripping with sarcasm. "Must be all about the letters, then."

Thomas, leaning back slightly, raised an eyebrow but didn't engage. Instead, he refocused the conversation. "The letters... they're more than just history. They paint a picture of a relationship that was tragically cut short. We're still trying to figure out exactly how it ended, but it feels... important."

Elena nodded, her excitement returning. "I think Abigail and Samuel's story should be a highlight of the exhibition when we reopen the manor. Their connection to this place is profound, and their story deserves to be told."

The group fell silent, contemplating her words. Sophie finally broke the tension, her voice soft but tinged with awe. "Wow, Elena. You've really been digging deep into this, haven't you?"

"Yeah," James added with a chuckle. "But it sounds like you and Thomas have been digging together."

Elena shot him a look but didn't respond to the jab. Instead, she pressed on, eager to shift the focus back to history. "We've only just scratched the surface, but these letters... they breathe life into the manor in a way nothing else has."

Thomas took the cue, standing and holding one of the old photos up to the light. "This place was their sanctuary. They would sneak in through the back entrance, meet in secret, and share music in this room." His voice softened as he traced the edges of the faded photograph. "You can almost feel them here. By the way, we have found some old photographs in the attic together."

Clara rolled her eyes, her earlier sarcasm still simmering just beneath the surface. "Sounds like more secrets. First the letters, now you're sneaking into rooms? You two sure have been spending a lot of time together."

Elena shot Clara a playful glare. "There's no conspiracy here, Clara."

"Oh, sure. No conspiracy," Clara quipped. "Just shared secrets and, I'm guessing, a lot of late-night research."

Sophie giggled while Aarav leaned against the wall, silently observing the exchange with raised eyebrows.

"I just think the letters add something... personal to the restoration," Elena continued, keeping her focus on the project. "They're not just artefacts. They're a connection to the people who lived here. Samuel and Abigail's love story gives this place a soul."

Thomas nodded, his eyes meeting hers briefly. "It changes the way we see the manor, doesn't it?"

"Exactly," Elena agreed, her voice more confident. "And I think we can use that. Their story can guide the way we design the exhibits. Make it more than just a house—it becomes a narrative, a living history."

Sophie, ever the life of the group, clapped her hands together. "Well, if we're going to be unearthing scandalous romances, I say we celebrate. To Abigail and Samuel!" Sophie smiled, glancing between them both. "Well, whatever secrets you two are keeping, you're definitely onto something. I say we make this story the heart of the exhibition."

Clara leaned back with a smirk. "I still think there's more going on than you're letting on. Secrets, love stories... sounds familiar."

Thomas cleared his throat, deflecting. "The focus should be on Abigail and Samuel. Their story deserves to be told."

Thomas leaned in closer to Elena as the others began to chat animatedly around the letters. "Is she always like that?" he said, his tone quieter now, more serious.

Elena nodded, her gaze distant as she watched the others. "It feels like she doesn't like me. She wanted my job. Also, I heard that she was into you..."

"I don't see why I would be into her. I prefer enthusiastic troublemakers to bullies," Thomas added softly, his voice carrying a weight of understanding that made her chest tighten.

Elena glanced at him, catching the flicker of

something unreadable in his eyes before he turned his attention back to the others. She wasn't sure what lay ahead—what secrets were still buried within the walls of the manor—but she knew one thing: she wasn't alone in uncovering them.

The team laughed and clinked their bottles, but Elena felt the weight of Clara's comments hang in the air. She glanced at Thomas and, for a moment, wondered if she was the enthusiastic troublemaker and, if so, if she'd like it.

James, ever the jokester, raised his beer bottle with a grin. "To secrets, then. And to figuring them all out—together."

As the night progressed, the conversation steered back toward ideas for the exhibition. The laughter and camaraderie grew, but the unspoken understanding between Elena and Thomas lingered beneath the surface—a connection forged not just by the manor's history but also by the feelings that pulled their hearts from their natural course, forgetting to beat separately, drawn irresistibly toward each other in silent unison.

A few cheers echoed around the room, and the tension that had hung so heavily moments ago began to dissipate. Someone produced a bottle of wine, and just like that, the solemnity of discovery transitioned into a spontaneous celebration.

The night carried on, the manor's old walls bearing witness to both its past and present lives, as Elena stood in the corner, letters in hand, wondering what Abigail and Samuel would think of them now.

CHAPTER 8

Elena's head throbbed from the remnants of last night's indulgence, her body heavy with the weight of sleep and the lingering effects of wine. She pulled the blanket over her head, hoping for a few more moments of peace. It was her day off, after all, and she had planned to stay in bed as long as possible.

A knock at the door shattered that plan.

Groaning, Elena flung the covers off and shuffled toward the door, still in her kitten-patterned pyjamas—an oversized shirt and shorts that were, admittedly, much shorter than she'd realised when she first put them on. She opened the door and was greeted by Thomas's raised eyebrow and a smirk that made her stomach flip.

He teased, eyes flicking down to her sleepwear. "Nice pyjamas."

Heat rushed to Elena's face, a deep blush spreading as she realised how ridiculous she looked. She crossed her arms over her chest, trying to act casual, but the teasing glint in Thomas's eyes only made her more self-conscious.

"I didn't know we were starting today," she muttered, ready to close the door on him.

"It's our day off, but we have an exhibition to prepare and a manor to restore," he reminded her with a playful lilt in his voice. "Besides, you need a shower. You kind of... smell like last night's wine." He chuckled, clearly enjoying her discomfort.

Her blush deepened. "You're the worst."

"I'll bring coffee," he offered with a grin. "How do you take it?"

"Half milk, two sugars," she said automatically, too flustered to argue.

"Got it. Be ready in half an hour," Thomas said, backing away but still watching her with amusement. "Oh, and Elena?"

She paused, her hand on the door.

"Make sure you're... decent this time," he said, flashing her a final smirk before turning away.

The door closed with a soft thud, and Elena let out an exasperated breath. He was impossible. Yet, as much as she wanted to stay in bed all day, she found herself rushing to get ready, eager to meet him at the manor.

Why did he have to be so irritating and... charming?

True to his word, Thomas appeared with coffee.

A short while later, Elena arrived at Ashford Manor, the faint scent of her shampoo clinging to her freshly washed hair. She found Thomas already waiting in the library, surrounded by stacks of old letters and diaries. He looked up as she walked in, his usual smirk softened but still present.

"Feeling better?"

Elena ignored his question and sat down opposite him, reaching for one of the letters. "Let's get on with it."

They began reading through the letters, each word drawing them deeper into Abigail and Samuel's story. Elena's voice grew softer as she read one particular entry aloud:

"My dearest Samuel, each day apart from you feels like an eternity trapped within these walls. Yet, when I steal away to our music room, where your notes still linger in the air, I feel the promise of your return."

Thomas, who usually maintained a distance from the emotional weight of their work, seemed unusually quiet, his eyes fixed on the page. He tapped his fingers lightly on the table as though lost in thought.

"This is more than just history," Elena murmured, half to herself. "It's... their whole life, right here in these words."

Thomas leaned back in his chair, arms crossed. "It's a dangerous line, though, isn't it? Showing too much of their personal life, revealing every little detail. Where do we stop? Where does history become gossip?"

Elena frowned, sensing the beginning of another debate. "It's not gossip, Thomas. This is their legacy. They wanted to be remembered, wanted their love to be known."

"But what about the cost?" Thomas pressed. "Doesn't it feel a little like we're prying into something sacred? Making their private lives public for the sake of an exhibition?"

Elena shook her head, her frustration building. "People need to see this, Thomas. They need to understand the depth of their love and the sacrifices they made. How else will they connect with the story? It's more than just dusty documents—it's real."

Thomas sighed, rubbing his hand across his face. "I get it. I do. But I also think we owe them some respect. There's a line, and we need to make sure we don't cross it."

Elena softened, realising that despite their differences, they both wanted to honour Abigail and Samuel in their own way. She looked down at the letter in her hand, her fingers tracing the faded ink. "Maybe there's a balance," she said quietly. "We can tell their story without turning it into a spectacle. We can show the love, the pain, without... exploiting it."

Thomas met her gaze, something unspoken passing between them. He nodded. "Yeah. Maybe you're right."

The silence that followed was heavy but comfortable, the weight of their discussion hanging in the air as they continued to work. For the first time, Elena felt the shift—something between them was changing. Slowly, subtly, but undeniably there.

As they poured over the documents, the hours slipped away unnoticed. The letters revealed more about Abigail and Samuel's secret meetings, their plans to escape to France, and the growing tension between duty and desire. Each entry was a glimpse into a world that had been hidden for too long.

Elena's fingers hovered over the map Samuel had sketched, the route of their planned escape etched in delicate, hopeful strokes. The paths they had plotted seemed almost to breathe with their dreams and desperation. "They were so close," Elena murmured, her voice tinged with a mix of awe and sadness. "They could have made it."

Thomas moved closer, his presence both reassuring and unsettling. He leaned in slightly, peering at the map over her shoulder. "But they didn't," he said softly, his tone carrying an edge of practicality that contrasted sharply with Elena's emotional depth. "If they had made it, we would have found some indication of that success. But there's nothing. The diary stayed."

Elena's eyes flicked up to his, searching for any hint

of empathy. "Are you sure? Maybe they didn't have a chance to write anything after they left. Maybe they were caught right away."

Thomas shook his head, his expression thoughtful but resolute. "Elena, think about it. She was writing almost every day. If they had managed to leave, she would have taken the diary with her. She would've documented every moment, every detail. The absence of any such records tells us something significant happened."

The realisation struck Elena hard. Her shoulders slumped slightly, the weight of the unspoken truth settling in. "So what happened?" she asked, her voice barely above a whisper. The vulnerability in her tone was palpable, a mix of frustration and a desperate need for answers.

Thomas's gaze was steady, but there was a flicker of something in his eyes—an acknowledgement of her emotional struggle tempered by his own sense of duty. "Something major. An event that would have stopped them in their tracks. They wouldn't have just disappeared without a trace if they'd escaped."

Elena's frustration bubbled to the surface. "We can't just accept that they failed without understanding why. There has to be something—some record, some mention of their attempt. We owe it to them to find out."

Thomas took a step back, his tone growing firmer. "And we will, but let's not get ahead of ourselves. This village is small, and any scandal would have made waves. The city archives are our best bet for finding concrete evidence."

Elena's eyes narrowed slightly. "And what if there's nothing? What if we dig through the archives and come up empty-handed? What then?"

Thomas met her gaze evenly, the tension between them crackling in the air. "Then we'll know we've done everything we can. But I believe there's something there—something that'll give us the full story."

The sharp edge in Thomas's voice only heightened the tension, but Elena's determination was unwavering. "We need to go now," she said, her voice resolute. "Every moment we delay is another moment these people's story remains unfinished."

Elena read another letter, this one more emotional than the last, and paused, glancing up at Thomas. His eyes were focused on her, more serious than she had ever seen them.

"What?" she asked, feeling the tension between them shift slightly.

Thomas shrugged, a small smile tugging at the corner of his lips. "You're good at this."

"Reading?" she quipped, trying to defuse the strange, lingering energy between them.

"Finding the heart of it," he said softly. His voice was almost too quiet like he wasn't sure he wanted her to hear.

Elena felt her pulse quicken at his words.

"We're getting closer," she said, more to herself than to Thomas, trying to stop the tension in her shoulders. "We're going to figure this out, one letter at a time."

"We will find it. But not with empty stomachs. On top of that, you probably haven't eaten this morning."

"Yes, a very unpleasant person woke me up and ordered my presence."

Thomas laughed. It was the first time Elena heard him laugh. She couldn't stop herself from finding it adorable.

Thomas smiled slightly, his usual teasing edge gone, replaced with something more genuine. "We will."

"Anyway, I'm starving. There's a pub not far from here—fancy grabbing lunch?"

Elena blinked, caught off guard. Lunch? With Thomas? The idea felt so... normal. And yet, her stomach fluttered at the thought. It wasn't really a date, but it wasn't just work either. The thought of spending time with him outside of the manor, away from the restoration, sent her mind spinning in a way she wasn't prepared for.

"Sure," she said, trying to sound casual, though her heart was beating faster than she'd like to admit. "Why not?"

He gave her a crooked smile, one that made her feel

both excited and nervous. It was just lunch. No big deal.

As they prepared to leave, the air between them was charged with a blend of shared purpose and unspoken tension. Their professional rivalry had sharpened into a personal conflict, driven by their differing views on how to handle the past. But beneath that tension was a mutual respect that neither could fully ignore.

They headed out of the manor together, the quiet of the early morning broken only by the distant sound of birds and the soft crunch of gravel underfoot. Each step felt heavy with anticipation and uncertainty. The day ahead promised answers but also the potential for deepened conflict and revelation.

As they reached the edge of the village, the weight of their task loomed large, but as did the unspoken connection that was beginning to form between them —one forged in the crucible of shared discovery and the relentless pursuit of truth.

But as they left the manor behind, walking side by side under the brightening sky, Elena couldn't shake the feeling that maybe, just maybe, something between them had changed—and not just because of the letters they were uncovering.

CHAPTER 9

Thomas held the door open for Elena as they stepped into the small village pub. The low hum of conversation, the crackling of a nearby fireplace, and the warm scent of roasted meats filled the air. Wooden beams lined the ceiling, and framed photographs of local fishing boats adorned the walls. The pub had the charm of a place untouched by time— dark wooden tables, mismatched chairs, and the clink of pint glasses as the bartender poured drinks behind the bar.

Thomas lingered at the door for a moment, watching Elena with a growing sense of confusion. Something had shifted between them, though he couldn't quite put his finger on it. He closed the door and followed her to a table by the window, where the sunlight streamed in, casting a soft glow on their faces.

They sat down, and a waitress came over to take their

order. Thomas ordered a pint of local ale, while Elena opted for a simple cup of tea and a sandwich. As soon as the waitress left, Elena, not one to waste time, pulled out her mobile.

She scrolled through the images, her fingers pausing on a particular set. "I took pictures of Abigail and Samuel's last letters," she said, her eyes scanning the screen. "And Abigail's final entries from her diary."

Thomas raised an eyebrow, a smirk forming. "This morning, you didn't want to get up. Now you're pulling out letters over lunch?"

Elena shot him a look, half-amused, half-defensive. "I couldn't help it. We're close, Thomas. Every word matters."

He leaned back, crossing his arms. "Fine, fine. Let's see what you've got."

Elena handed him her phone, showing a letter from Samuel written in a frantic hand. The parchment was torn and worn as if it had been clutched too tightly in desperate moments. Together, they read the words aloud, their voices low, melding with the background hum of the pub.

"Abigail, I know that our troubles may seem never-ending at the moment. However, I want to believe that there is hope for us and that our love will transcend all our trifles."

Thomas's eyes met Elena's. "He's not just talking about their families here. He's talking about a life together.

This isn't just some fleeting romance."

Elena nodded, her focus returning to the screen. "They were planning to defy everything—their families, the expectations... Even the law, probably. Look at this next one."

She flipped to another letter from Samuel, outlining a plan for their escape. His words were filled with urgency, describing in bold but almost naïve terms how they would flee to France under the cover of night.

"This was their rebellion," Elena said, her voice tinged with admiration. "They weren't just star-crossed lovers. They were trying to change their fate. To rewrite everything."

Thomas tapped the table thoughtfully. "I wonder if they ever believed they could pull it off. It's one thing to dream about escaping, but actually doing it? Running away with nothing but a promise and a plan... It's dangerous, reckless."

"But it's also beautiful, in a way," Elena countered. "They believed in something bigger than themselves. That takes courage."

Thomas tilted his head. "Or desperation."

"Maybe both," Elena admitted. "But it's why we're still talking about them now, isn't it? They weren't just any couple—they were willing to risk everything."

As Elena and Thomas continued to flip through the digital images of the letters, a comfortable silence settled between them. The pub's lively atmosphere seemed to fade into the background as the weight of Abigail and Samuel's words took centre stage.

Elena spoke first, her voice soft but steady. "In these later letters, Abigail's writing shifts. She starts to share more than just their plans to escape. She pours her heart into the letters, her fears, her hopes... It's like she's leaving a map of her soul for Samuel to follow."

The letter was written in Abigail's familiar, graceful hand, but the words within struck with a force Elena wasn't prepared for. *"Samuel, I can hardly bring myself to write these words..."* it began before delving into a confession so unimaginable it made Elena's breath hitch. Abigail's father—her own father—intended to marry her. The lines were laced with Abigail's horror, her fear, and a desperate plea for Samuel to understand the danger they were truly in. This wasn't just about a forbidden love anymore. It was a battle for Abigail's freedom, her very soul. Elena could feel the weight of every word, the suffocating dread that must have haunted Abigail as she wrote them, trapped between a father's twisted control and a love she could never publicly claim.

The letter closes with a desperate appeal to Samuel, urging him to remember their dreams of a future unfettered by societal chains. She implores him for patience and fortitude, promising to find a way to be together despite the formidable barriers. The urgency of her situation is palpable, leaving the reader to ponder the high cost of love in a time when personal happiness was often a secondary consideration to familial duty.

As Elena reads through Abigail's fervent words, she feels a profound connection to the young woman's plight, bridging centuries of societal change yet finding striking parallels in their emotional landscapes. This letter, a testament to forbidden love's trials, compels Elena to delve deeper into the manor's secrets, searching for any hint of how Abigail and Samuel might have navigated these treacherous waters.

The urgency in Abigail's letter resonated deeply with Elena. She became more determined to uncover the fate of the lovers, feeling an increasing responsibility to bring their hidden narrative to light. She hoped to find a happier ending in the historical record than the one hinted at in the desperate lines of Abigail's letter.

Thomas nodded, scanning one of the letters she'd pulled up on her phone. "Her words almost read like poetry—so much emotion, but with an urgency that feels incredibly modern…"

Elena leaned in closer, pointing to a particular passage. "'I have family in Paris who may be willing to give us sanctuary for the meantime. I am willing to do whatever it takes to be with you, Samuel, even if it means leaving all of this behind.'"

Thomas let out a low whistle. "That's not just desperation. That's commitment."

"She's willing to abandon her entire life," Elena murmured, her fingers tracing the words on the screen as if she could touch the past. "Everything she's ever known—her family, her home. And yet, for her, it's worth the risk."

Thomas sat back in his chair, rubbing his chin thoughtfully. "And Samuel—he responds with such fierce loyalty. But there's a different tone to his letters. He's protective, almost to a fault."

Elena clicked through to one of Samuel's replies, reading aloud: "'I don't want you to leave everything and sacrifice your life for me. I want you to be happy, but I also want you to be safe.'"

Thomas looked up, his gaze catching Elena's. "He's torn. He wants her, but he knows the cost. And it's like he's already preparing for the worst."

"Exactly," Elena said. "It's not just about escaping anymore. It's about survival—both of them knowing what they're up against and still choosing to be together."

Their conversation deepened as they pored over more letters. Abigail and Samuel's correspondence had transformed from mere logistical discussions into something far more personal. Their letters were now their lifelines, the essence of their rebellion against a world that wouldn't let them be together.

"They weren't just planning," Thomas mused. "They were fighting back in their own way. Every word was like a move on a chessboard, a strategy to outwit the world."

Elena leaned back in her chair, her eyes distant as she spoke, "I keep imagining what Abigail must have felt standing in that music room with Samuel, finalising their escape. It wasn't just fear driving her. It was something else—something stronger."

Thomas looked at her, intrigued. "What do you think it was?"

"She must have felt exhilaration too. I can picture her standing there, her hands clasped in his, knowing they were about to defy everything. There's a quiet strength in her letters, but when they made that decision, it must have all come to the surface. I imagine her eyes, a mix of fear and excitement, meeting his, silently asking if they were really doing this."

Thomas nodded, leaning forward. "And Samuel, do you think he hesitated at all? Maybe for her sake?"

"No," Elena said thoughtfully. "If anything, I think he tightened his grip on her hands, reassuring her. He was ready, just like she was. By that point, they weren't just two lovers plotting an escape—they were partners in rebellion. I can almost hear him whispering to her, promising to protect her, to see this through no matter what."

Thomas smiled slightly. "You're turning this into quite a dramatic scene."

"Well, isn't it?" Elena countered, a spark in her eyes. "They were standing there, knowing they were about to risk everything. Abigail, who had always written about her dreams of freedom, was finally about to act on them. And Samuel—he wasn't just a musician anymore. He was leading her, both of them, into something dangerous and thrilling."

"Do you think they ever doubted themselves?" Thomas asked, his voice softer now.

Elena paused, considering. "Maybe in those quiet moments after they'd hidden the letters back in the piano. Maybe then, they'd feel the weight of what they were doing. But when they left that room, I think they were resolute. They stepped out into the night, fully committed, leaving behind the sanctuary where they'd whispered their vows and sealed their fate."

Thomas tapped the table gently as if reflecting on her words. "It's incredible to think how much of their story was hidden within those walls. Their love wasn't just defiant; it was transformative."

Elena met his gaze, her voice quiet but firm. "They didn't know it then, but what started as a rebellion became something much deeper. It became a story of survival and courage. And that room—Abigail must have felt it too—wasn't just a place anymore. It was a witness to their love, their decisions, everything they stood for."

Thomas sighed, running a hand through his hair. "I wonder what it felt like for them, walking out of that room, knowing they'd either find freedom or lose everything."

"They didn't know," Elena replied softly. "But they were willing to risk it anyway. And you? What do you think Samuel was feeling?"

Thomas's brow furrowed as he began to picture Samuel's experience. "I imagine Samuel sitting alone, unfolding one of Abigail's letters," he said, his voice thoughtful. "His hands were probably trembling a bit, knowing what was at stake, but he was determined not to let fear consume him. Those words she wrote—about her father's demands, about the expectations chaining her to someone else—must have hit him hard."

Elena nodded, intrigued by how Thomas was immersing himself in Samuel's thoughts. "He wasn't just reading her words; he was feeling every ounce of her despair and urgency."

"Exactly," Thomas continued, leaning in. "But instead of breaking under that pressure, it ignited something in him—a fire, a kind of fierce resolve. He probably sat there in the dim light of a candle, writing his response with every fibre of his being. It wasn't just a love letter anymore. It was a manifesto. A declaration that their love wouldn't be another casualty of the world's demands."

Elena could almost see it herself now. "He must have planned their meetings meticulously, down to every detail. In those shadowed corners of the manor, they weren't just sharing stolen kisses; they were strategising. Samuel sketching out escape routes, maybe on scraps of paper—small maps of hope they dared to dream of, illuminated only by the stars."

Thomas's voice softened. "And those meetings... every one of them became more than just moments of affection. They were dangerous, calculated risks. But also... necessary. Samuel wouldn't let anything stand in their way."

Elena leaned back, a soft smile playing on her lips as she glanced at Thomas. "You're really good at this," she said, her tone teasing yet sincere. "Imagining all the details of their escape... it's like you've done this before."

Thomas chuckled, shaking his head. "Well, there's a reason for that." He paused, glancing away for a moment as if debating whether to continue. "I never told you, but I was kind of in a similar situation once. Not exactly the same, but close enough."

Elena's eyebrows lifted, intrigued. "You? Really? What happened?"

He sighed, the weight of old memories surfacing. "I was a teenager, upper class. There was this girl—she was lower class. We were in love, or at least I thought we were. My parents were completely against it, of course. They had all these expectations and plans for me to go to university, and they thought that a girlfriend, especially someone lower class, older, already working without a college degree, wasn't a good idea."

Elena leaned in closer, her curiosity piqued. "What did you do?"

"For a while, we talked about escaping, running away together. But in the end, we never did. My parents found out and sent me to a boarding school—Eton, of all places," he added with a wry smile. "I never spoke to her again after that."

"That must have been hard," Elena said softly, sensing the weight of regret in his words.

"It was," Thomas admitted, his voice quiet. "But we were young. I think, in some way, I knew it wouldn't last. Still, I never forgot about her. Funny enough, I follow her on Instagram now." He grinned, trying to lighten the mood. "No mystery to be uncovered there, though. She's happily married, living in the Cotswolds, and has two kids."

Elena laughed, shaking her head in disbelief. "So, you're telling me you were part of a forbidden romance?"

"Something like that," Thomas said, his grin widening. "Except mine didn't come with secret letters or grand plans of rebellion. Just teenage drama and disapproving parents."

"You're full of surprises," Elena said, her gaze lingering on him for a moment longer than usual. "But I guess it explains why you understand Samuel so well."

Thomas nodded, the playful air around him softening again. "Yeah, I guess it does. Samuel wasn't just fighting for love; he was fighting against everything he was supposed to be. And… I get that."

Elena smiled, their connection deepening in the shared vulnerability. For a moment, she allowed herself to reflect on how much closer they had become —not just as colleagues but as something more. The walls between them were thinning, their pasts and their work drawing them together in ways neither had anticipated.

CHAPTER 10

As Elena and Thomas chatted over their drinks, the sound of footsteps signalled the arrival of a cheerful, chubby woman wearing a well-worn apron. Her rosy cheeks beamed beneath a mess of dark curls streaked with grey. With a thick Scottish accent that rolled off her tongue like a melody, she exclaimed, "Och, if it isn't ma cutie!"

Elena looked up, startled by the sudden burst of affection aimed at Thomas. The woman—clearly a local—beamed as she set their meals down, her plump hands moving with the practised ease of someone who'd spent a lifetime running a pub.

"This one's in here more often than the whisky barrel," Moira said with a hearty laugh, patting Thomas on the shoulder. "Can't keep him away. I swear he's in love with me!" She winked playfully at Elena, her eyes twinkling with mischief.

Thomas, never one to miss a beat, grinned back.

"Guilty as charged, Moira. In fact, I brought Elena today for a bit of moral support. Thought it was time I popped the question."

Moira threw her hands up dramatically, gasping in mock offence. "Pop the question? Thomas, ye daft thing! I'm already spoken for—married tae the chef, no less!" Her laughter rang out, filling the pub with warmth.

Amused, Elena shook her head, finding it hard to picture this light-hearted side of Thomas. Before she could dwell too long on it, Moira's expression shifted, her jovial nature giving way to curiosity. "I heard ye two talking about Abigail Ashford earlier," she said, her voice lowering. "There's an auld tale 'round these parts about her."

Elena leaned forward, intrigued, while Moira continued, her accent thickening as she delved into the story. "They say her fiancé and his father had her locked up, so she couldnae run off wi' her lover to France. Poor lad waited for her by the shore. When she didn't come, he threw himself into the water. Never seen again."

"Is it true?" Elena asked, feeling a chill despite the warm atmosphere of the pub.

Moira shrugged, her smile creeping back. "Who's to say? It's a legend, aye, but a good one for the tourists. They say his ghost still haunts the place where he drowned, and if ye want tae bless yer love, ye lay a cardboard heart for him. Silly nonsense, but folk love a bit o' drama."

With that, Moira gave them a wink and turned to go, her apron swishing as she bustled off to tend to other tables. "Enjoy yer meal, loves," she called over her shoulder. "And mind the ghosts don't follow ye home!"

As soon as Moira left, Elena leaned toward Thomas, her eyes shining with sudden urgency. "Thomas, this confirms it! Abigail's father must have imposed that fiancé on her, and she planned to escape to France with Samuel. If those details are right, maybe the rest of the legend is true too!"

Thomas, calm as ever, shook his head slightly. "Elena, it's just a local legend. Stories like this always get blown out of proportion. They change over time, and details get exaggerated."

But Elena wasn't backing down. "If the newspapers don't mention anything about a lady eloping with a commoner, the local archives will surely have a record of her arrest! If Abigail was locked up, there has to be documentation. We could even find out the name of the fiancé, and once we have that, we can check the marriage registers. It could lead us to exactly what happened."

Thomas's sceptical expression softened as her excitement spread. "That's true. The archives might give us what we need."

Elena nodded eagerly, her thoughts racing. "We were

already planning to go there this afternoon to look through the old newspapers. But now, with this information, we'll have even more to search for. We're not just chasing rumours anymore—we're getting closer to the truth. We might finally touch on what really happened that night."

Elena hurried through the rest of her meal, eager to rush off and dive into the archives. Thomas watched her with a smirk, clearly amused by her determination.

Before they could leave, the door to the pub swung open, and Clara walked in. Clara's words lingered in the air as she approached their table, her voice casual but sharp. "Thomas, I thought you left early this morning," she said, a smirk playing on her lips.

Without a flicker of shame or hesitation, Thomas simply nodded. "Yeah, I had to go investigate further with Elena," he replied matter-of-factly, as if there was nothing more to explain.

But for Elena, it felt like the ground beneath her had shifted. Something inside her was breaking apart. She realised, with a hollow ache, that she had started to like Thomas—maybe even love him. And now, it was clear. He was sleeping with Clara. That smirk, that familiarity—it was all too obvious. He was probably hoping to do the same with her. The betrayal hit her like a punch to the gut, and it took every ounce of her will to hold back the tears burning in her eyes. Shocked, disappointed, and utterly crushed, she kept her face calm, her emotions buried beneath a practised mask.

Clara, clearly pleased with herself, gave a knowing glance between the two of them. "I suspected something like this," she said with a petty smile. "Still together, huh? Well, I'll see you tonight anyway." With that, she walked off to grab a table, leaving a trail of discomfort in her wake.

Elena, determined not to let her heartbreak show, forced herself to stay composed. "Well," she said, her voice steady despite the turmoil inside her, "I'm a historian. I don't need an architect for archival research." Her hands trembled slightly as she reached into her bag to pay for her meal, eager to leave the pub and escape the pain swelling inside her.

Thomas, oblivious to her distress, insisted, "I'm coming with you. I want to find out the truth as much as you do."

Elena's control faltered for just a second, her voice cold as she replied, "I, too, would've liked to know the truth." Her words were sharp, loaded with meaning that Thomas didn't seem to grasp, but she wasn't going to explain. Not now.

She stood up, forcing a smile that didn't reach her eyes. "Since you're the one who invited me," she added coolly, "you can pay the bill." Without waiting for a response, she turned and walked toward the door, her heart heavy with the sting of betrayal.

Elena stepped out of the pub and into the cold embrace of the Scottish air. The sky was a slate grey, heavy with the threat of rain, and the dampness in the air seemed to seep into her skin. She walked over to a nearby park, its small patch of grass dotted with bare trees and a few benches. A biting wind cut through her coat, sending a shiver down her spine. She found a bench under an ancient oak, its gnarled branches twisting against the pale sky, and sat down, pulling her jacket tighter around herself.

The air smelled of wet earth and sea salt, a constant reminder of the looming North Sea just beyond the village. The cold clung to her cheeks, stinging her skin, but she barely felt it as she stared at her phone. The archives wouldn't open until 2 p.m.—twenty more minutes to sit with her thoughts, to wallow in the ache that gnawed at her insides.

Her fingers moved absentmindedly over the screen, scrolling through information, but her mind was elsewhere, circling the betrayal she hadn't seen coming. Thomas and Clara. The way Clara had smirked, so smug, so certain. And Thomas—he hadn't even tried to deny it. Not that he owed her anything, she reminded herself bitterly. They weren't together. But still, she had allowed herself to hope, to imagine that maybe there was something real between them.

God, how could I have been so stupid? The thought echoed in her mind. She'd fallen for him, for his charm, for the way he looked at her when they worked together. She had mistaken professional rivalry for something deeper, something personal. And now, sitting on this cold bench with the damp air clinging to her skin, she felt utterly foolish.

She wanted to cry, to let it all out, but the tears wouldn't come. Instead, a hollow feeling settled in her chest, a kind of dull, relentless ache. The park around her was empty; the only sound was the occasional rustling of leaves in the wind and the distant cry of a seagull. Even nature seemed indifferent to her pain.

She checked her phone again. Fifteen minutes. Enough time to feel sorry for herself a little longer. *Why did I even care so much?* she wondered, but the answer was painfully obvious. She hadn't just liked him—she'd begun to care for him. And now it felt like the rug had been pulled out from under her. The cold, the damp, and the solitude of the park felt like an extension of her own heart: empty, aching, and alone.

As Elena walked briskly through the park, her mind still tangled in the aftermath of her emotional revelation, a sudden, sharp realisation hit her. *Oh my God,* she thought, her eyes widening in disbelief. *I came here with Thomas in his car!*

She glanced at her phone again and noted the distance to the archives. It would take her about ten minutes to walk there.

Determined to shake off her melancholy, Elena stood up and took a deep breath, the chilly air filling her lungs. As she began her walk, her mind shifted focus. *If I can't have my own beautiful love story,* she thought resolutely, *then I'll make sure Abigail and Samuel's is remembered properly.*

Her steps quickened, the cold air brisk against her face. With each stride, the sense of betrayal began to fade, replaced by the familiar rush of her investigative spirit. The drive for uncovering the truth about Abigail and Samuel reignited her ambition. She would find out what truly happened years ago and bring their story to light, no matter how painful it might be.

By the time she reached the archives, her heart was steady again, her resolve hardened. If love wasn't in her future, she would make sure their story— one of love and tragedy—would be honoured and remembered. The archives awaited, and with renewed purpose, Elena pushed open the doors, ready to delve into the past.

CHAPTER 11

Elena pushed open the heavy wooden door of the archives, which groaned like it hadn't been oiled since the 18th century. The librarian, a spindly man with a grey beard that looked like a family of squirrels might be nesting in it, glanced up from his desk, his spectacles perched precariously on the tip of his nose.

"Good afternoon," Elena said, forcing a bright smile as she waved her Historical Society of Scotland company membership card in front of him. "I'm here to access the newspapers and official papers from the end of the 18th century."

The librarian took her card with the slow deliberation of someone inspecting a rare artefact. He squinted at it, flipped it over, and then held it up to the light as if it might reveal some hidden treasure. After what felt like an eternity, he nodded gravely. "Everything's digitised now for preservation," he announced, as though revealing the secret to eternal life. He pointed to a computer terminal at the far end of the room. "Just use that terminal over there. The papers you need are all scanned in."

Elena's smile faltered, but she nodded enthusiastically. "Great, thank you so much." She darted over to the terminal, her heart racing as if it were in a race against time.

She settled into the chair, which creaked ominously under her weight and began to navigate the computer. Her fingers fumbled over the keyboard, but she was so focused that she barely noticed. She shot a quick glance over her shoulder, only to see the librarian still peering at her through the gap in his office door, looking as if he were waiting for a dramatic reveal.

Determined to ignore the librarian's curious gaze, Elena turned her attention back to the screen, mentally preparing herself for the treasure hunt that lay ahead.

Elena's smile faded slightly as she took in the setup. "Thank you. I haven't used this system before. Do you have any tips on how to search for specific documents?"

The librarian's eyes lit up with the enthusiasm of a showman. "Ah, the system!" he exclaimed. "It's quite advanced, you know. Took me months of negotiations with the town hall to get it. They were convinced that the old microfilm was good enough. But I fought tooth and nail for this state-of-the-art software. It's got more capabilities than you can shake a stick at. You can search by keywords, dates, or even specific phrases. And it's all stored in the cloud—well, as much as a cloud can hold!"

Elena's patience wore thin as he continued his lengthy exposition, describing each feature of the system in excruciating detail. She was dying to tell him that this was already possible fifteen years ago, and nothing was new about it, but she smiled politely.

"You can filter results by relevance or date, and there's an advanced search option if you know how to use it. But don't worry, it's user-friendly once you get the hang of it," he said as if he had just unlocked the mysteries of the universe.

Elena forced a polite smile, trying to mask her frustration. "That's very helpful, thank you. I'm sure I'll figure it out."

The librarian gave a satisfied nod and started to drift away, only to turn back with another burst of enthusiasm. "And if you need any assistance, just give me a shout. I'm here all day, and I'm always happy to discuss the merits of this incredible software!"

Elena nodded quickly, her smile now strained. "Got it. I'll let you know if I need anything."

With that, she made her way to the terminal, her mind already racing with the need to find the right documents as quickly as possible. The librarian's voice faded into the background as her determination to uncover the truth about Abigail and Samuel sharpened her focus.

Elena began by typing "Ashford" into the search bar, hoping to narrow down the results. As the documents loaded, her screen was inundated with pages of articles, many of which were not relevant. Her frustration mounted as she scrolled through headline after headline. The name "Ashford" was everywhere, but finding the specific details she needed felt like finding a needle in a haystack.

Determined, Elena refined her search using additional keywords: "Abigail" and "engagement". She set parameters to limit the search to dates around 1798 and focused on articles mentioning Lady Abigail Ashford directly.

After several attempts, Elena found what she was looking for. The article dated January 1798 read:

"In a dramatic scene at the local church, Lady Abigail Ashford was seen in a heated confrontation with her father, Sir Ashford. The young lady, accompanied only by a young musician, was the centre of controversy. Sir Ashford is reported to have threatened to confine his daughter to the manor permanently, raising suspicions of ongoing tensions at home."

Elena's heart sank as she read the article. The image of Abigail standing alone against her father's wrath struck a chord with her. The thought of Abigail being confined, her freedom stripped away, made Elena's chest tighten with sympathy and sorrow. She could almost feel Abigail's desperation, her courage in the face of an oppressive father, and the pain of being torn away from Samuel. Elena felt a pang of empathy, as if Abigail's suffering resonated with her own struggles in navigating the expectations of her profession and personal life.

The second article, dated April 1798, was a stark contrast:

"The engagement of Lady Abigail Ashford to Sir Crampton has been announced, much to the astonishment of the local society. Despite Sir Crampton's recent financial ruin, the match is set to be celebrated with grandeur. This decision comes amidst ongoing speculation about Lady Ashford's previous relationship with a young musician."

Elena furrowed her brow, perplexed. Why would the local society be astonished by this engagement? Was the love story between Abigail and Samuel well-known among the townsfolk? The notion of this "grand celebration" seemed to mock Abigail's earlier plight. Elena began jotting down possible reasons for the astonishment:

Was Abigail and Samuel's relationship so scandalous that it became public knowledge?

Were there rumours or whispers about the true nature of the engagement that were now coming to light?

As she continued to read, Elena's curiosity grew. The timing of the engagement, coming so soon after Abigail's confrontation with her father, felt suspicious. Was Abigail being forced into this marriage to salvage her family's reputation or to align with powerful interests?

Elena scrolled back to an older article dated December 1796:

"In a disheartening turn of events, Sir Crampton has lost all his fortune in ventures in the Americas."

The revelation about Sir Crampton's financial situation only deepened Elena's confusion. She pondered why a wealthy man like Sir Ashford would choose to marry his only daughter to a financially ruined suitor. What qualities did Sir Crampton possess that were so valuable that they transcended monetary considerations? Elena began to write down her thoughts and questions:

What could Sir Crampton have that even money couldn't buy? Charisma, connections, or perhaps a strategic advantage?

Was there something in the late 18th century that was out of reach, even for someone as wealthy and influential as Sir Ashford?

Did Sir Ashford have personal or political motivations that made this marriage a strategic necessity?

Elena's mind raced with possibilities. Could it be that Sir Ashford saw an opportunity in this marriage to consolidate power, or was there an element of revenge or manipulation involved? She felt an increasing sense of urgency to uncover the truth behind these decisions.

Another article Elena found, dated May 1798, provided further insight:

"The entire town converses about the forthcoming marriage of of Lady Abigail Ashford and Sir Crampton with all indulging in countless speculations as to what this union might foretell, yet everyone agrees it will be the wedding of the century. However, whispers among the elite suggest that Lady Ashford's father used the marriage as a strategic move to strengthen his own position in society, despite Sir Crampton's impoverished state. This move appears to be a calculated effort to consolidate power rather than a genuine romantic union."

Elena's frustration grew as she read about the societal machinations behind the wedding. The realisation that Abigail had been used as a pawn in a game of social positioning was both heart-wrenching and infuriating. Elena felt a deeper connection to Abigail's plight, recognising how her own professional struggles often felt like a game of societal expectations.

The last document she accessed was the arrest record from May 21, 1798:

"Under the orders of Sir Ashford and her fiancé, Sir Crampton, Lady Abigail Ashford was detained on charges of hysteria. The report describes her as screaming and crying, appearing utterly desperate.

She was imprisoned for the night before being released without further charges."

Elena's heart ached as she read about Abigail's arrest. The image of Abigail's despair, confined and desperate, mirrored the pain Elena felt from her own recent revelations. The sense of betrayal and helplessness was palpable, and Elena felt a renewed resolve to see Abigail's story through. She scribbled down her final thoughts:

How could Sir Ashford and Sir Crampton justify such cruelty? What was so critical about this marriage that it necessitated Abigail's suffering?

What would make someone's fate so tragic and manipulated, and how can history shed light on this injustice?

As Elena was absorbed in her research, her phone buzzed with a message from Sophie.

"Hey, Elena. You are not going to be happy…"

Elena sighed, feeling the weight of the day pressing on her. "Tell me."

"I heard someone from our team mention your love story exhibit idea to the Historical Society of Scotland. They're coming on Monday to see if it's a good idea."

Elena's heart sank further. The pressure was mounting, and she felt overwhelmed. "I've found more clues, but I'm more lost than ever. I need time to piece this together."

CHAPTER 11

"I'll come pick you up and call the team. We can work on it tonight and get everything sorted for the exhibition tomorrow," Sophie offered.

"No, don't bother them, it's Saturday night. I'd prefer to work on it myself," Elena said, her voice steady despite the turmoil inside. She would rather avoid seeing Thomas and Clara today. "I'll be at the archives until they close. I appreciate the offer, though."

Sophie chuckled on the phone. "It's almost 7 p.m. I'm surprised they haven't pushed you out yet! I'll come over to pick you up and help if you need it. See you in ten minutes."

Elena hung up, feeling a mix of relief and resignation. The weight of Abigail and Samuel's story seemed heavier now, but she knew she couldn't let it falter. She packed up her notes and printed the documents she had found, and her mind raced with the need to focus on the exhibition and honour Abigail's tragic tale.

Just before disconnecting the computer, she did a last research, this time using the "obituary" category. "May 21, 1798 to May 25, 1798" and " Samuel" were the keywords.

No man named Samuel had died that week. The legend was wrong. Elena smiled. There was still hope, after all!

As she stepped into the chilly evening air, Elena was

resolute. She would confront the challenges head-on, not just for the exhibition, but for the truth of Abigail and Samuel's story. In doing so, she hoped to find some semblance of peace and purpose amidst the chaos of her own emotions.

CHAPTER 12

The cobblestone streets glistened from an earlier drizzle, the streetlamps casting a golden glow on the old stone buildings that lined the town's main road. The town itself was a picture of Scottish charm—narrow alleys, smoke curling up from chimneys, and the faint scent of peat in the air. Here and there, the sound of laughter escaped from the warm glow of the small pubs tucked between the shops, their wooden signs swinging in the breeze.

Elena quickened her pace, her boots clacking against the stone as she made her way toward the edge of the street. The wind picked up, tugging at her hair and sending a chill down her spine. She spotted Sophie's SUV before she heard the honk—a familiar, cheerful beep that cut through the quiet of the town. Elena hurried to the SUV, forcing a smile as she opened the door and slid inside.

"Hey there!" Sophie said, her usual cheeriness radiating through the small space as she put the car in gear. "You ready for some food? I was thinking Moira's pub—it's been ages since I've had a good meal there."

Elena stiffened at the mention of the pub, her stomach churning. Seeing Thomas—and Clara—again was the last thing she wanted tonight. She hadn't even processed what had happened earlier. The thought of facing them both made her throat tighten with anxiety.

"Actually," she said quickly, her voice a little too sharp, "I'm not really in the mood for Moira's. I don't really like the food there."

Sophie glanced at her, raising an eyebrow but still smiling. "Really? But it's the best around! What's not to like about Moira's?" She slowed the car as she reached a red light, then looked more closely at Elena. "Okay, spill it. What's really going on?"

Elena's grip tightened on her seatbelt, her heart pounding as she debated what to say. Sophie wasn't the type to let things slide, and she was too perceptive to buy a flimsy excuse about food. Elena swallowed hard and looked out the window. The streetlights blurred into streaks of gold against the darkened sky.

"I just... I don't want to see Thomas," she admitted, her voice barely above a whisper.

Sophie's eyes softened in understanding, though her smile never wavered. "Ah, I see. So there's a trouble in paradise, huh?"

Elena let out a bitter laugh, her throat tight with emotion. "There's no paradise, Sophie. There's nothing." She fought back the tears threatening to spill over, pressing her lips together to keep them at bay.

Sophie, ever the optimist, didn't miss a beat. "Alright then, no Moira's tonight. How about we grab a Munchy box instead? We can head back to the manor and eat. I've been craving one of those greasy delights for ages!"

A few minutes later, they were back on the road, the Munchy box warming Elena's lap. The greasy smell of chips, battered sausages, and fried pizza filled the car, but Elena's stomach remained in knots.

The rich scent of fried food filled the car, but Elena barely noticed. Her stomach twisted—not with hunger, but with the same gnawing anxiety that had been bothering her all day.

"Sorry again for making you settle for a Munchy box instead of Moira's cooking," Elena said, staring out the window. Her voice was faint as if she was apologising for something far deeper than fast food.

Sophie shot her a sideways glance, grinning. "Settle? Please, don't worry, Elena! Sometimes, greasy chips and fried pizza are just what the doctor ordered. Besides, you know I love a good Munchy box."

Elena smiled faintly but didn't respond. Sophie, ever

cheerful, drummed her fingers on the steering wheel, humming to the rhythm of the radio. But as the silence stretched on, Sophie's intuition kicked in.

"Elena, you alright?" she asked gently, her tone losing its usual carefree edge. "You've been quiet since we left."

Elena bit her lip, feeling the weight of her thoughts pressing down harder. She took a deep breath, her voice trembling as she spoke. "I think I'm stupid."

The words spilt out before she could stop them, hanging in the air between them. Sophie's eyebrows shot up in surprise, and without a second thought, she pulled the car to the side of the road, cutting the engine. The town's faint hum faded, replaced by a thick silence.

"Stupid? Are you serious?" Sophie turned fully in her seat to face Elena, her eyes wide with disbelief. "Elena, you are not stupid. Why would you even say that?"

Elena shifted uncomfortably, her fingers nervously picking at the edges of the Munchy box. "For thinking... for thinking I could handle everything. The manor restoration, the letters, the past... I thought I was in control, but now everything feels like it's slipping through my fingers. I'm drowning in it."

Sophie's expression softened. "You've got a lot on your plate, Elena, but that doesn't make you stupid." She leaned in, her voice firm but full of warmth. "You're one of the smartest people I know. You're brilliant.

You've dedicated yourself to uncovering the history of that place and giving it life again. Do you know how many people could do what you're doing? Not many, I can tell you that."

Elena stared down at her hands, feeling a mixture of shame and relief. "I don't know, Sophie. Lately, I just feel like I'm messing everything up. Like I'm not good enough."

"Not good enough?" Sophie's voice rose an octave in disbelief. "Elena, you've been piecing together an entire historical puzzle, all while handling the pressures of the restoration. You've uncovered secrets that have been buried for centuries! You're dedicated, passionate, and kind. That's not something just anyone can do."

Elena blinked, touched by her words but still uncertain. "I just... I don't know if I can keep doing this. It feels like I'm falling short everywhere."

"Elena, listen to me." Sophie's tone grew more serious, her voice steady and comforting. "You are doing amazing things. I mean it. And yes, sometimes it feels like everything's crashing down, like you're failing—but you're not. You're learning, you're growing. And you're doing it all with heart. That's what matters."

For a moment, Elena was silent, feeling the words sink in. She hadn't realised just how much she needed to hear that. Sophie's unwavering support felt like a lifeline, grounding her in the midst of her doubts.

Elena sighed, her voice trembling slightly. "I thought there was something between me and Thomas, but now I'm starting to think I was wrong. He's been spending time with Clara."

Sophie's eyebrows arched in surprise. "Clara? Are you sure?"

Elena nodded, her gaze distant. "I'm sure. Clara walked in while Thomas and I were finishing lunch. She was so casual about it, like they were a couple. Thomas seemed comfortable, like he had no reason to hide anything. It was... clear."

Sophie was quiet for a moment, processing this. Then she said, "I don't know, Elena. That doesn't sound like something Thomas would do, not so openly, at least. Maybe it's just a misunderstanding."

Elena shook her head. "It felt real, Sophie. Clara had this smirk on her face, and Thomas didn't exactly look surprised to see her. It was like they had their own secret world."

Sophie stopped the car at a red light, her attention fully on Elena. "Look, I get that it's upsetting. But you can't let one moment cloud everything. People can be complicated, and sometimes what we see isn't the whole story."

Elena's eyes were brimming with unshed tears. "I don't know if I can handle this, Sophie. I thought there was something real, something... hopeful. But now I just feel like a fool."

Sophie reached over, placing a comforting hand on Elena's shoulder. "Elena, listen to me. You're not a fool. You're someone who dares to hope, to care deeply, and to invest in what you believe is true. And that's not something to be ashamed of."

Elena looked at Sophie, her voice breaking. "I just thought... I thought Thomas and I had a chance. But if he's with Clara..."

Sophie's expression was resolute. "It's not about Thomas. It's about you. You've got so much to offer— your passion, your intelligence, your kindness. Don't let this one situation make you doubt yourself. You deserve someone who sees you for who you are and appreciates you."

Elena's heart swelled at Sophie's words, her eyes glistening. "Thank you, Sophie. I needed to hear that."

Sophie smiled warmly. "Of course. And remember, whether it's Munchy boxes or Moira's, we're doing this together. We'll figure it out. And who knows? Maybe there's someone better out there who's just waiting to see how amazing you are."

As they continued their drive to the manor, Elena felt a glimmer of hope amidst her turmoil. The road was long and uncertain, but with Sophie's support, she felt less alone.

When they arrived at the manor, Sophie turned to Elena with a grin. "Let's get inside and dive into those new finds. There's nothing like a bit of archival digging to take your mind off things."

Elena nodded, feeling a bit more grounded. "Sounds good. Let's get to work."

With that, they carried their Munchy boxes inside, ready to tackle the mysteries that awaited them. And as Elena looked around the familiar surroundings of the manor, she felt a renewed sense of purpose bolstered by her friend's unwavering support.

CHAPTER 13

Sophie and Elena settled into the old, worn chairs of the manor's dining room, the dim light from the chandelier casting long, dancing shadows over the heavy oak table. The air was thick with the scent of aged wood and faintly musty tapestries, a sharp contrast to the greasy, fragrant Munchy box they'd dropped in the centre of the table. It looked almost comically out of place amidst the room's sombre grandeur. Sophie, grinning, speared a fry dripping with melted cheese and leaned forward.

"Probably the fanciest Munchy box these walls have ever seen," Sophie quipped, popping the fry into her mouth with a satisfied hum. She chewed, then leaned in, wiping her fingers on a napkin. "So, what did you find today?"

Elena reached into her bag, pulling out the documents she'd carefully gathered from the archives. As she spread them across the table, the flickering light made the edges of the papers seem older, as though time itself clung to them.

"Well, it's a lot," she began, her voice weighed down by the significance of her discoveries. She slid the first paper toward Sophie—a police report from May 21, 1798. The faded ink seemed to whisper of long-forgotten injustices. "This is a record of Lady Abigail being arrested for hysteria. Her father, Sir Ashford, and her fiancé, Sir Crampton, had her detained. The report says she was 'screaming, crying, and appeared utterly desperate.' They released her the next day, no formal charges... but this was the night she was supposed to elope with Samuel."

Sophie frowned, her mouth half full of chips. "Hysteria? So... they just locked her up because she was upset?"

"Essentially, yes. Back then, 'hysteria' was often a catch-all diagnosis for any behaviour seen as 'unacceptable' for women, especially if they defied men in power. She was going to run away with a commoner. Her fiancé and father probably didn't have any issue with pretending she had hysteria."

"Lovely," Sophie muttered sarcastically, wiping her mouth with the back of her hand. "Go on."

Elena moved to the next paper, a newspaper article from May 1798. "This one talks about Abigail's wedding. It was called the 'wedding of the century,' but it wasn't a love story. Apparently, her father orchestrated the whole thing to consolidate his power despite Sir Crampton being financially ruined."

Sophie's eyebrows shot up. "Wait, so her dad knew the guy was broke but still made her marry him? Why?"

"It was all political," Elena explained, flipping to another article dated December 1796. "Sir Crampton lost his entire fortune in ventures in the Americas. It was a huge public scandal."

Sophie scooped up more fries, shaking her head in disbelief. "And Abigail had no choice in all this?"

"Exactly. Her father used her as a pawn. And it gets worse." Elena gestured to another document, an article from January 1798. "This one mentions a confrontation at the church. Abigail was seen arguing with her father, and she wasn't alone—she was with a young musician. Sir Ashford threatened to confine her to the manor after that."

"A musician? Do you think that was Samuel?" Sophie asked, leaning closer.

"That's what I'm starting to think," Elena said, her eyes dark with thought. "Abigail was clearly involved with this man, and her father didn't approve. But somehow, a few months later, she suddenly became engaged to Sir Crampton. The April 1798 article describes it as a surprise to everyone, especially considering Crampton's financial collapse."

Sophie put down her fork, her brow furrowed. "So, let me get this straight. Abigail was in love with a musician, her dad didn't approve, and after some kind of public scandal, she ended up engaged to a man who was basically bankrupt? And then, when she got upset, they locked her up?"

"That's the gist of it," Elena nodded. "It looks like Abigail's father was desperate to save face and maintain his influence, even if it meant sacrificing her happiness. He wouldn't allow her daughter to elope with Samuel, so he imprisoned her for the night. And who knows what happened to Samuel, the musician? I know he didn't die that night, but I wasn't able to do more research, not knowing his family name."

Sophie sighed, shaking her head. "What a mess. Poor Abigail. No wonder she was screaming." She paused, eyes narrowing thoughtfully. "But why would her father go to such lengths to marry her off to someone with no money? Even if it was a political move, it doesn't add up."

"I've been wondering the same thing," Elena said. "There's something more to this story, something we're missing. Abigail's life seems to have been dictated by everyone around her, but the details aren't all there yet."

Sophie took a long breath, nodding slowly. "Sounds like you're going to need to dig deeper. Maybe there's more to find out about Samuel or why Sir Ashford was so determined to push Abigail into this marriage."

"Exactly. And with the wedding approaching, she must have felt completely trapped. She was trying to fight back, but everything was against her."

CHAPTER 13

Sophie pushed the Munchy box aside and leaned in. "So, what's the next step? What else can we find about Samuel or the circumstances around the marriage?"

Elena sighed, staring at the papers before her. "The next step is figuring out where Samuel went. If there's any trace of him after that confrontation, I need to find it. And I need to understand what was really at stake for Sir Ashford—what did he gain from this marriage?"

The room fell quiet for a moment, the weight of the past pressing in on them as they sat in the grand dining room, surrounded by the manor's history. Sophie broke the silence with a determined smile.

"Well, whatever we find, I'm here to help. We're getting to the bottom of this, one way or another."

Elena returned her smile, a small flicker of hope lighting within her. "Thanks, Sophie. We've got a long road ahead, but we'll get there."

The remnants of their meal were scattered across the table, along with grease-stained napkins and empty Munchy boxes, adding an odd contrast to the grandeur of the dining room. The old space, though in the middle of being restored, still carried the echoes of history. Sophie leaned back in her chair, wiping her hands on a napkin, and turned to Elena with a serious expression.

"We need to start thinking about the pre-exhibition for the Historical Society of Scotland," Sophie said, her voice taking on a more focused tone. "If we don't give them something solid to work with, they might cut off our funding—or worse, stop our research."

Elena nodded, already feeling the weight of that pressure. "I've been thinking about that too. We need to craft something that'll grab their attention, something that ties Abigail's story to larger themes."

Sophie nodded. "Exactly. And what stands out to me, after all this research, is just how limited Abigail's choices were. It wasn't just her—it was every woman in her position, trapped by societal expectations and the power of men in their lives."

Elena sat up straighter, her mind racing. "What if we frame the exhibition around that? Make it about feminism, focusing on the constraints placed on women in the 18th century. Abigail's story is the perfect example of how women were used as pawns for political and social gain, without any real say in their own lives."

Sophie's eyes lit up. "Yes! We can emphasise the stark contrast between their public and private lives— the expectations forced upon them versus what they were really going through. Abigail's diary entries, the newspaper articles, all of it fits."

Elena looked around the room thoughtfully. "The dining room's almost finished. We could hold the pre-exhibition here, make it intimate and authentic."

Sophie's face brightened. "Perfect! And what if we

present the key entries from Abigail's diary and the newspaper articles like a menu?"

Elena smiled, starting to see the vision come together. "Yes, copies of the most important entries and documents placed at each setting, laid out as if they were dining here two hundred years ago."

Sophie tapped her fingers on the table, clearly inspired. "And we could even get Moira to help with the food. She could make a menu based on things that existed in 1798—authentic dishes that people like Abigail and her family would've eaten. That would add a real layer of immersion."

Elena grinned at the idea. "I bet she'd love to be involved. It'll give the whole thing a sense of authenticity that's hard to replicate."

"And it would make the Historical Society of Scotland feel like they've stepped back in time," Sophie added, her enthusiasm growing.

Elena chuckled, a wicked glint in her eye. "And I think we should make Thomas act as a valet. After everything, it's the least he can do."

Sophie burst into laughter, clapping her hands together. "That's brilliant! The look on his face when you tell him… priceless."

Elena leaned back, enjoying the idea. "I'll tell him it's part of the immersive experience. A lesson in 18th-century social dynamics."

"Exactly." Sophie giggled, still picturing it. "We'll have

the exhibit focused on feminism and women's rights, and he'll be playing the role of a servant. How fitting."

The two women exchanged amused glances, their laughter echoing in the quiet dining room. But beneath the humour, they were serious about the importance of their work. The pre-exhibition would be the key to continuing their research, and they were determined to make it not just a success but a statement.

CHAPTER 14

Monday arrived, shrouded in a dense mist that clung to Ashford Manor, giving the manor an air of silent anticipation. Elena gathered her team in the drawing room, feeling the weight of the day's importance settle heavily on her shoulders. Noon was approaching, and with it, the Historical Society of Scotland, who would decide if the manor's restoration was worthy of a grand exhibition.

Her team trickled in, their voices echoing off the high ceilings. Clara arrived with a clack of her sharp heels that seemed louder and more deliberate than necessary. James strolled in before Thomas entered last, his eyes briefly meeting Elena's before he turned his attention to the others. The tension between them was palpable, a remnant of the day they'd spent together, and Elena felt a pang of frustration mixed with a reluctant fondness she didn't fully understand yet.

Elena took a deep breath, trying to steady her nerves, and stepped forward to address the group. "Thank you all for coming," she began, her voice betraying a hint of the anxiety she felt. "The Historical Society of Scotland will arrive at lunchtime to evaluate our work and discuss the potential for an exhibition. It's crucial that we present a unified vision—both in terms of the manor's history and its future."

She distributed folders containing the finalised menus Sophie had meticulously worked on. As her team opened them, they found not just menus but also carefully inserted articles, diary entries from Abigail, and period-appropriate illustrations. Sophie's effort had turned the menu into an educational tool, merging the history of Lady Abigail's life with the presentation.

"Sophie's done an excellent job," Elena continued. "The menus not only replicate what we believe would have been served in 1798 but also incorporate historical notes about the Ashford family and Abigail's struggles, cleverly disguised as menu items. Our guests won't just be eating—they'll be learning. Sophie is currently at the pub with Moira, the owner, preparing a lunch that's a meticulous replica of a meal from 1798. She's working hard to ensure every dish reflects the period accurately."

Turning to the rest of the team, Elena addressed their tasks. "James, you and Thomas will handle the final check-up on the foundations. The building team finished last week, but we need to ensure everything is perfect." James nodded, and Thomas gave a curt, affirmative nod, though his expression was unreadable.

"Aarav," she said, "you'll continue working on the restoration of the central staircase." Aarav, as always, acknowledged her with a thumbs-up.

Finally, Elena turned to Clara, the last name on her list. Her stomach tightened, not just from the task at hand but from the lingering tension between them. "Clara, I need you to be with me and the Historical Society of Scotland during the luncheon. You'll be our expert on Scottish heritage and 18th-century local history. I want you to engage them in a discussion about the role of women in society during that period, particularly relating to the Ashford family and the broader social implications we're exploring."

Clara's smile was slow and sharp, her eyes glinting with a calculated edge. "Of course, I must be there," she said, her tone light but dripping with condescension. "I wouldn't want you to struggle through a conversation with such important specialists. Historical nuance can be quite a challenge for some."

Elena felt the jab, its sting sharp and personal. She refused to let Clara see her discomfort, though. She straightened her shoulders and forced a tight smile. "Thank you, Clara. Your expertise will be invaluable."

Without another word, Elena clapped her hands, breaking the tension. "Right, everyone. Let's get to work. We don't have much time."

As the team dispersed, Elena lingered in the drawing room for a moment, allowing herself a quiet breath. The manor felt heavy around her, its walls steeped in centuries of secrets. Abigail's presence seemed almost tangible, the story of her life clawing its way through the years, demanding to be told.

Clara's words echoed in her mind, but she pushed them aside, focusing on the task ahead. Her career—and the success of the exhibition—hinged on today's presentation. There was no room for petty rivalries.

As she made her way to the study, her mind was occupied with last-minute details when she heard the unmistakable sound of footsteps behind her. She tensed but didn't turn immediately. She knew who it was. When she finally glanced back, Thomas was approaching, his usual calm demeanour replaced by something that bordered on hurt.

"Elena," he began, his voice low, "why didn't you tell me about the things you found in the archives? The articles, the menus... they're right here." He held up the menu in his hand, the historical clippings and period-appropriate dishes displayed prominently.

Elena's heart skipped a beat. She had been processing the revelations about Abigail Ashford and Samuel alone, struggling with her feelings. Part of her had been reluctant to share, not just because of mistrust but because she had started to develop feelings for Thomas. The thought of him knowing everything felt... complicated.

She crossed her arms, meeting his gaze with a look that betrayed none of her inner turmoil. "You haven't told me everything either, Thomas."

His brow furrowed in confusion. "What do you mean?"

Before he could ask more, Elena lifted a hand, cutting him off. "Look, today is far too important for this. We'll talk later."

Thomas's eyes narrowed, his suspicion clear, but he let it go for now. "You're right. Later, then."

As he started to leave, Elena's lips curled into a sly smile. "By the way, you're going to play the role of a valet at the luncheon. Sophie's found you a suit. It's in the guest room."

Thomas's eyes widened in surprise. "A valet? You can't be serious."

Elena's smirk deepened. "Oh, I'm dead serious. Ashford Manor had valets in 1798, didn't it? Consider it a step back in time."

His confusion shifted to disbelief. "Wait—you actually want me to...?"

Elena shrugged, feigning innocence. "It suits you. You'll blend in perfectly. Besides, Clara mentioned you were always good at multitasking."

The jab landed. Thomas's eyes widened further, his expression a mix of shock and realisation. Before he could respond, Elena turned on her heel and walked away, leaving him momentarily speechless.

By noon, the Historical Society of Scotland arrived—eight in total, dressed in sombre yet stylish attire. Elena welcomed them at the entrance of Ashford Manor, her nerves a tight coil beneath her composed exterior. She guided them through the grand entrance hall, past Aarav's staircase restoration, and into the elegantly set dining room.

The table was a meticulous blend of past and present: silverware gleaming, plates adorned with delicate historical motifs, and menus neatly placed at each setting. Every detail was designed to evoke 1798.

As the guests took their seats, Thomas entered, dressed in a sharp, vintage-inspired suit that made him look convincingly like a valet. He moved with quiet efficiency, serving drinks and appetisers with a professionalism that impressed Elena. Despite their recent tensions, he was showing respect for her work in this unusual role.

Clara seized the opportunity to dominate the conversation. "Women in 18th-century Scotland had no legal rights," she said, her voice smooth and authoritative. "They couldn't own property or enter into contracts, yet they were pivotal to society—noblewomen as pawns in marriage alliances, peasant women as the backbone of rural economies. They often wielded hidden power behind men's ambitions."

Elena felt a flicker of irritation at Clara's subtle air of

superiority but knew better than to engage in a public battle. When Clara paused, Elena took her chance.

"Abigail Ashford's story exemplifies that hidden power," Elena said, her voice steady. "Confined by her father's expectations and society's demands, her pursuit of a relationship with Samuel speaks volumes about her strength. This isn't just a love story—it's a narrative of rebellion. It's about breaking free from imposed roles. The emotional and historical elements here have the potential to captivate a modern audience."

The Historical Society of Scotland representatives listened, their initial polite interest shifting to genuine engagement as Elena spoke.

"The combination of lost love and historical context gives this exhibition dual appeal," Elena continued. "It's not just a story; it's a reflection of the limitations placed on women and their courage to push against those boundaries."

The lead representative, an older woman with sharp eyes, nodded approvingly. "You've done well, Ms. Carter. The historical research is compelling, and I agree that the emotional elements will draw in a wide audience. We're prepared to make this exhibition the centrepiece of the manor's reopening—provided you continue your research and ensure every detail is accurate."

Elena felt a surge of triumph, though she kept her expression composed. "We'll ensure that the research deepens and that the exhibition reflects the complexity of Abigail Ashford and Samuel's history, as well as women in the 18th century."

After the luncheon, as the company members toured the manor, they were particularly impressed by the central staircase and the meticulous attention to detail in each room. As they neared the exit, the lead representative turned to Elena with a smile.

"Truth be told when Clara mentioned a far-fetched project involving a portrait of the manor's inhabitants, we were concerned. When Clara contacted us, she suggested that the project might benefit from... a different approach, from someone with more expertise in Scottish history."

Elena's smile tightened, her eyes narrowing slightly as she processed the information. The representative's words were unmistakable: As a historian specialising in Scottish heritage, Clara had attempted to undermine her by positioning herself as a better candidate for the role.

"We're pleased to see that the project has been executed with such thoughtful consideration," the representative continued. "Your dedication to both the historical accuracy and emotional depth of the exhibition is truly commendable."

Elena took a steadying breath, her expression calm despite the underlying tension. Clara's attempt to sabotage her efforts was now laid bare, but Elena focused on the success of the day and the approval from the Historical Society of Scotland.

As the company finally departed, leaving Elena and her team to bask in their success, Sophie sidled up to her, a mischievous glint in her eye. "Clara's a real piece of work, isn't she?"

Elena couldn't help but smile, her expression a mix of triumph and camaraderie. "She is, but it doesn't matter. We won."

Sophie grinned, linking her arm with Elena's. "That we did. And if Clara has anything to say about it, she can have a seat in the back row. We made history today."

Thomas caught her gaze. He was no longer in his valet suit but had reverted to his usual attire, looking both relieved and uncertain.

"You were amazing today," he said softly. "But why did you really make me dress up like that?"

Elena's eyes twinkled mischievously. "Because you're more than just a historian, Thomas. Sometimes, to truly understand the past, you need to experience it in all its detail—even if that means dressing up as a valet."

Thomas chuckled, shaking his head in disbelief. "You have a knack for surprises."

"Just consider it part of the learning experience," Elena replied. "I'm glad you were here today. It made a difference."

Victory was indeed sweet. Elena took a moment to reflect on their hard-earned success, feeling a profound sense of relief and satisfaction. As the team celebrated, she chose silence over confrontation. There would be other battles to fight. For now, she savoured the satisfaction of a job well done and the unwavering support of her friends and colleagues after weeks of work.

CHAPTER 15

The evening sun cast a warm, golden glow over Ashford Manor as the team gathered in the grand hall to celebrate their hard-won success. Laughter and the clinking of glasses filled the air, mingling with the rich scents of the catered dishes that had replaced the formal dining setup. Elena beamed as she observed her team—James, Sophie, Aarav, Thomas, and Clara—all gathered in animated conversation.

Sophie stood on a chair, gesturing dramatically as she recounted the day's highlights. "I mean, did you see the look on their faces when they walked through the dining room? It was priceless!"

James nodded, raising his glass. "And the food—Moira really outdid herself. The replica dishes were spot on."

Elena clapped her hands, drawing the group's attention. "I'm so proud of everyone. This is exactly the kind of engagement we need. Everyone

—engineers, architects, historians—came together to make this presentation a success."

Thomas, who had finally shed his valet attire, stood with his arms crossed, a smile tugging at the corners of his mouth. "You were right, Elena. The immersive experience was something else. I didn't think I'd enjoy it, but it actually worked."

Elena's eyes sparkled with delight. "I'm glad you think so. I was worried that the historical details might feel too far removed from what everyone else is doing here."

Clara, who had been quietly sipping her drink, spoke up. "I'll admit, the idea of combining historical accuracy with the presentation was more effective than I anticipated."

"Now that the Historical Society of Scotland is on board," Elena said, "we need to start brainstorming for the next steps. We have the opportunity to really showcase Abigail's story and the broader historical context."

Sophie nodded enthusiastically. "I was thinking we could use the different rooms to highlight various aspects of Abigail's life. Maybe the library could focus on her written correspondence and personal reflections. The drawing room could present the political and social pressures she faced."

James, who had been listening intently, suggested, "And the great hall could be used to display some of the major events, like the scandal and the wedding. We could set it up to look like an 18th-century gathering."

Elena's eyes lit up with inspiration as she interjected, "What if we created a special experience in the music room? Given its historical significance to Abigail and Samuel, we could transform it into a setting that mirrors their secret meetings. Imagine this: we could play a waltz and use shadow play to make the light dance across the room, creating the illusion of a hidden couple. It would be like bringing their story to life."

Aarav's eyes widened with interest. "That sounds incredible. The shadow play could be a really unique way to engage visitors and immerse them in the romance of the time."

Sophie clapped her hands excitedly. "I love it! It would add a touch of magic to the presentation and highlight the personal aspect of Abigail's story. Plus, it's a beautiful way to show how their love transcended the constraints of their time."

James nodded thoughtfully. "And the waltz could be a beautiful, poignant touch. We could even consider incorporating some period-appropriate music to enhance the atmosphere."

Thomas, who had been quietly listening, spoke up with a grin. "It's a brilliant idea, Elena. It captures the essence of Abigail and Samuel's secret romance perfectly. It'll make the music room stand out and give visitors a sense of intimacy and nostalgia, as well as the fact there were hidden, with the light disappearing and reappearing."

Aarav chimed in, "The central staircase could be an exhibit in itself, highlighting the architectural changes made over time and its significance in the manor's history."

Thomas, now more engaged, added, "And we could create an interactive display in the study, where visitors can explore the different layers of Abigail's story through a touch-screen or augmented reality. It could make the history come alive."

Elena looked around, her heart swelling with pride. "These are fantastic ideas. I'm thrilled to see everyone so involved. It's clear that we're not just working on a project; we're creating an experience that blends history with the present."

As the evening wore on and the team's energy began to wane, Clara took her leave with a curt nod, her presence less conspicuous now. The remaining team members continued their discussion, fine-tuning their ideas and revelling in their success.

Eventually, the room began to empty, and Elena found herself alone with Thomas. The last of the celebratory chatter faded into the background as Thomas approached her with a thoughtful expression.

"Elena, could you wait a moment?" Thomas asked, his tone more serious than before.

Elena looked at him, her curiosity piqued. "Of course. What's up?"

In her head, Elena already knew what was up. Thomas wanted to know why she had been avoiding him. He took a deep breath, his gaze steady. "Why didn't you tell me what you found in the archives?"

Thomas hesitated for a moment before speaking. "You don't trust me anymore? I enjoyed doing research with you. When I saw the articles and the menus you'd put together, I understood that, apparently, it wasn't the same for you."

Elena sighed. She was fuming. How dare he accuse her of not wanting the same as him when he was the one flirting with her while obviously having an affair with Clara. "It's been a lot. I wanted to share everything with you, but I was struggling with how to do that, especially given the tensions between us. It felt complicated."

Thomas's expression grew puzzled. "I don't understand. What tensions?"

Elena couldn't help but laugh, though it was a humourless sound. "What tensions? Thomas, you were flirting with me, or so I thought, and then at the pub, Clara comes and says that you left her early that morning! Of course there's tension!"

Thomas looked taken aback. "Wait, what? I'm not involved with Clara."

Elena's eyes narrowed, her voice edged with hurt.

"How can you say that? Clara mentioned you left her early that morning, the same morning you came to my hotel with coffee. How do you explain that?"

Thomas's shock was evident. "Elena, that's not what you think. I left early to get the coffee and see you because I genuinely wanted to discuss the project. Clara and I—there's nothing going on between us."

Elena's tone was laced with anger. "Really? Because you've acted so casually about everything. You didn't even try to explain yourself. You just said we'd talk tonight."

Thomas's face was a mix of confusion and regret. "I didn't realise how it must have looked. I should have been more open with you. I sleep at the same hotel as Clara. In a different room, obviously! We just take our coffee together in the morning before coming to work."

Elena took a deep breath, her emotions still raw. "Well, it did cause a misunderstanding. I've been trying to handle this on my own, and your actions only added to the stress. I need you to be honest with me, Thomas. We're in this together, and I need to trust that you're fully committed to the project and to clear communication."

Thomas's expression softened as he took a step closer, his eyes locked onto Elena's. "Elena," he said, his voice low and filled with raw, unfiltered emotion. "I'm not just committed to this project—I'm committed to you. I need you to know that. I've been trying to figure out how to tell you this because you drive me crazy, but I can't hold it back any longer."

Elena's heart raced as she met his gaze, the tension between them crackling with an undeniable electricity. Her emotions were a tangled mess of longing, desire, and uncertainty. She felt a profound connection with Thomas, and the intensity of his words made her pulse quicken. The vulnerability of the moment revealed how deeply she cared for him and how much she had been yearning for him to be honest and open.

Thomas reached out, cupping her face gently in his hands. "I'm not just in this for the history or the restoration," he continued, his voice husky with desire. "I'm here because I want you. Every time I see you, every time we're together, it's like I'm drawn to you in a way I can't explain."

Elena's breath hitched as Thomas's fingers brushed against her skin. The thrill of his touch made her shiver, amplifying the raw need that had been simmering beneath the surface. "I thought you were with Clara," she said, her voice trembling slightly with a mix of hope and doubt.

Thomas shook his head, a dark intensity in his eyes. "I've never been with Clara. I've been thinking about you—about us. You're everything I've wanted, and I can't ignore it any longer. And right now, I don't want to hear any other name than yours. Or mine, sighed by you."

Without another word, Elena closed the gap between them, his lips crashing onto hers in a kiss that was both urgent and tender. The kiss was a revelation, a collision of pent-up emotions and desperate need. Elena felt her doubts melt away as the passion between them ignited.

Thomas responded fiercely, his hands gripping her shirt as their bodies pressed together. The kiss deepened, becoming a desperate exploration of shared passion and longing. Elena's senses were overwhelmed by the heat of his touch, the strength of his arms, and the sheer intensity of his desire.

Thomas's hands moved with a decisive, almost primal urgency as he began to undress her, his touch sending shivers down her spine. Each article of clothing was discarded with a mix of tenderness and fervour until Elena stood before him, vulnerable and electrified. Her heart pounded not just from excitement but from the emotional weight of this moment, the culmination of their shared journey.

With a determined look, Thomas lifted Elena effortlessly into his arms. "There's a place in this manor," he murmured against her ear, his breath hot and intoxicating. "A place where love has been born for centuries."

Elena felt a moment of hesitation, but it was fleeting. The connection she felt with Thomas was so strong that any lingering doubts were quickly overshadowed by the overwhelming desire to be with him. As they moved through the grand corridors of Ashford Manor, the thrill of their intimacy felt exhilarating, a promise of something profound and enduring.

Elena's eyes fluttered shut as she nuzzled against him, her heart pounding. "Yes," she breathed, her voice thick with anticipation. "Take me there."

Thomas carried her through the grand corridors of Ashford Manor, his stride confident and purposeful. The music room, with its historical charm and intimate ambience, awaited them. He set her down gently on the queue of the grand piano, his eyes never leaving hers.

In the soft, flickering light of the room, Thomas's gaze held an intensity that spoke of deep desire and profound connection. As they came together in the quiet sanctuary of the music room, their bodies entwined, it was clear that their passion was not just a fleeting moment but a reflection of something much deeper—a love that transcended time and echoed the historical romance they had been unravelling together.

As the night unfolded, the music room became their private world, a place where their emotions and desires mingled with the echoes of Abigail and Samuel's own love. In the intimacy of the moment, they found solace and connection, their bodies and hearts aligning in a dance of raw, unfiltered emotion.

Afterwards, as they lay together, Elena felt a mix of contentment and vulnerability. The intensity of their connection left her breathless and awed. She reflected on their journey, recognising the strength of their bond and the evolution of their relationship from professional partners to something far more intimate. This reflection added an extra layer of emotional depth to their encounter.

As she nestled against Thomas, Elena felt a profound sense of belonging and unity. The future of their relationship seemed bright, filled with hope and the promise of shared experiences. For now, she savoured the satisfaction of a connection that was as deep and enduring as the historical romance that had brought them together.

CHAPTER 16

Thomas stirred first, his arm draped lazily over Elena, who lay nestled beside him. He blinked against the soft morning light filtering through the music room windows, a slow, contented smile spreading across his face.

"Morning," Elena murmured, her voice soft and warm.

Thomas grinned, leaning in to press a kiss to her shoulder. "Morning," he replied, his tone light but filled with affection. "We should probably avoid making this a habit... unless we plan on adding 'piano concert' to the manor's exhibits."

Elena chuckled, turning her head to look at him. "Well, it wouldn't be the worst scandal to come out of Ashford Manor."

He ran his fingers through her hair, tucking a loose strand behind her ear. "Last night... was more than I expected."

"It was," she agreed, her gaze softening. "I'm glad we finally talked. It's... nice, not having that tension between us."

Thomas nodded, his expression growing thoughtful. "Feels like we've crossed a line, doesn't it? And not just with..." He gestured vaguely, his grin returning. "You know."

Elena smirked, sitting up slightly, still wrapped in the warmth of their night together. "Yeah, I know." She leaned over to press a kiss to his cheek before standing up, feeling a sudden rush of excitement. "Actually, there's something I've been dying to show you."

Thomas's brow furrowed in curiosity as she hurriedly fetched her bag. He watched her with interest, the last traces of sleep falling away as her eagerness became infectious.

"Remember I told you about the archives?" Elena began as she settled back beside him, now holding a small stack of old newspapers. Her eyes gleamed with excitement as she laid them out carefully between them.

"Crampton, Abigail's fiancé—he wasn't always the wealthy man he was supposed to be. Look at this," she handed him the first article. "This one's from before the engagement."

Thomas scanned the headline. His brows furrowed. "He lost his fortune?" he asked, surprised.

"More than a year before the engagement was

announced," Elena said, her voice quickening. "It doesn't make sense—why would her family push the match when he was ruined?"

Thomas's eyes flickered with interest as he took in the implications. "There had to be something more going on," he murmured. "What else did you find?"

Elena handed him another paper dated January 1798. "Here. This one's even more telling."

She watched as he read it, his expression shifting from curiosity to shock.

"In a dramatic scene at the local church, Lady Abigail Ashford was seen in a heated confrontation with her father... accompanied by a young musician..." Thomas read aloud, trailing off. "Samuel."

Elena nodded. "Abigail and Samuel were trying to escape. That's what I think. But her father wasn't having it—he threatened to lock her away."

Thomas's jaw clenched, and he set the paper down. "So she was forced into the engagement with Crampton... What else?"

Elena's hands trembled with anticipation as she showed him the next article. This one was from April 1798, the announcement of Abigail's engagement to Crampton. "Look at how they describe it—everyone knew about her relationship with Samuel, yet the engagement went forward."

Thomas read it, his face hardening. "Despite Sir Crampton's recent financial ruin... the match is set to be celebrated with grandeur."

Elena's gaze softened as she reached out, resting a hand on his arm. "There's more," she said quietly, her voice trembling as she spoke. "I found an arrest record... It was the night she was supposed to escape with Samuel."

Thomas looked up at her sharply, shock and anger flickering in his eyes. "What?"

Elena took a deep breath and handed him the final piece of the puzzle—the arrest record from May 21, 1798. "This is the night they were supposed to run away together. Samuel must have been waiting for her, but instead... they arrested her. They stopped her before she could get to him."

Thomas scanned the document, his face hardening with every word. "Under the orders of Sir Ashford and her fiancé, Sir Crampton, Lady Abigail Ashford was detained on charges of hysteria..."

"They labelled her hysterical just to lock her away," Elena said, her voice filled with quiet fury. "She was imprisoned for the night, and after that... she was forced into the engagement. Samuel probably had no idea what happened to her."

Thomas's hands shook slightly as he set the paper down. "They made sure she had no choice," he murmured, his voice raw. "She was trapped—first by her family, then by Crampton. They used everything against her."

CHAPTER 16

Elena, still sitting on the piano, reached for her bag and pulled out a well-worn notebook. She flipped through the pages, each filled with hurried notes, sketches, and questions that had haunted her since she began delving into Abigail's story. Her pen had drawn lines connecting names, dates, and places, forming a web of intrigue.

"I wrote these down after I visited the archives," she explained, her voice calmer now, though the weight of what she had uncovered still lingered. "These are the questions that keep coming back to me, and they hold the key to understanding what really happened to Abigail."

She held the notebook open to a page filled with questions. Thomas glanced at it before looking up at her, listening intently.

"Was Abigail and Samuel's relationship so scandalous that it became public knowledge?" she began, her voice thoughtful. "Were there rumours or whispers about the true nature of the engagement that were now coming to light? Was Abigail being forced into this marriage to salvage her family's reputation or to align with powerful interests?"

Elena paused, her brow furrowed as she considered the implications of each question. "These are the things that could have easily been answered back in 1798. But now, we're left piecing it together. I plan to visit the archivist again... he's been kind to me, and I think he might have access to more than he's shared so far."

Thomas nodded, taking in her words. Then, with a thoughtful expression, he said, "You know, I knew a Crampton back in my Eton days."

Elena blinked, surprised. "Really?"

"Yeah," Thomas replied, frowning slightly as he thought back. "We weren't close, but I remember he came from an old family with deep roots. I could give him a call... maybe he knows something about his ancestor, Sir Crampton. It's worth a try."

Elena looked at him with renewed interest. "That's a great idea. There's something about Crampton that doesn't add up. What could he have had back then that even money couldn't buy? Was it charisma, connections... or maybe something more strategic?"

Thomas rubbed his chin, his mind working through the possibilities. "Maybe Sir Crampton had access to something or someone powerful. And Sir Ashford... perhaps he wasn't just saving face. Maybe there were political motivations, something bigger at play."

Elena's eyes narrowed in thought. "Exactly. Was there something in the late 18th century that was out of reach even for someone as wealthy as Sir Ashford? What could have made this marriage a necessity?"

They sat in silence for a moment, the weight of the unanswered questions hanging between them. Finally, Elena sighed and flipped to the last page in her notebook, where she had jotted down two more questions.

"For these last two," Elena said, her voice softer, "I think we need to take a broader approach. Maybe even save them for the manor's opening."

Thomas raised an eyebrow. "The manor opening?"

Elena took a deep breath, collecting her thoughts before she began to explain to Thomas. "You see, Thomas," she said softly, her voice carrying the weight of her historical knowledge, "in the late 18th century, women like Abigail weren't seen as individuals with their own desires or autonomy. They were, more often than not, treated as pawns in a larger social or political game. Marriages, especially among the aristocracy, were rarely about love—they were alliances. Abigail's marriage to Sir Crampton was less about her own wishes and more about what her father, Sir Ashford, needed to secure his family's power, influence, or reputation."

Thomas listened intently as Elena continued, her voice growing more impassioned. "The cruelty Sir Ashford and Sir Crampton showed towards Abigail wasn't an isolated incident. Women of her stature were expected to sacrifice their happiness for the 'greater good' of their family. Abigail wasn't just a victim of her father's ambition—she was a symbol of how many women's fates were dictated by the men in their lives."

She paused, her gaze focused on the papers scattered on the piano. "This question 'how could they justify such cruelty?' isn't just about Abigail. It's about how women were treated in that era. Their suffering was often seen as acceptable or even necessary if it served a larger purpose. That's why I want to explore this question when we open the manor to the public, to show people how history often erased the voices of women like Abigail. How their stories of manipulation and oppression were hidden behind the facade of family duty or social expectation."

Elena looked at Thomas, her eyes filled with resolve. "By telling Abigail's real story, we're also shedding light on the broader issue of how women were systematically oppressed, controlled, and denied autonomy. Her suffering is part of a much larger pattern that existed during that time."

Thomas's brow furrowed as he processed Elena's words, his voice quiet but thoughtful. "So, it's not just about Abigail being forced into this marriage—it's about the whole system that treated women like property, isn't it? They didn't stand a chance. Her father and Sir Crampton probably thought they were doing what was expected of them, but it destroyed her."

Elena nodded, her eyes bright with determination. "Yes. We're restoring more than just the building. We're telling the story of the people who lived here and these questions"—she pointed to the notebook—"go beyond Abigail. They ask something more universal."

She glanced at him, the passion in her voice unwavering. "It's about how many women in history were trapped in the same way, their lives manipulated for political or social gain. Abigail's story gives us a way to explore those broader themes of control, sacrifice, and how women were silenced."

She handed him the notebook, and Thomas read aloud:

"What was so critical about this marriage that it necessitated Abigail's suffering?"

Elena spoke softly, "What would make someone's fate so tragic and manipulated, and how can history shed light on this injustice?"

Thomas considered the questions for a long moment before looking at her. "You're thinking of entrusting this part to Clara?" He sounded surprised.

Elena smiled faintly. "Yes, I am. I know she wants my position, but she's the only other historian on the team. And let's be honest—Clara will do an excellent job because she wants to look good in front of the Historical Society of Scotland."

Thomas smirked, amused by Elena's logic. "True. Clara is meticulous when it comes to her reputation."

"Exactly," Elena said. "She'll present these questions in a way that shines a light on the broader implications of Abigail's story. And if we're going to do this right, we need her. The public deserves to know the full truth."

Thomas closed the notebook, handing it back to Elena. His expression softened, filled with admiration for her determination. "You're right. This isn't just about the past. It's about making sure people understand what really happened—and why."

Elena smiled, feeling the warmth of his support. "We're telling a story that's been buried for too long."

Elena slipped into her shirt, buttoning it quickly before smoothing her hair with her fingers. "You need to check on the framework today. Make sure it's solid," she said, glancing at Thomas as he tugged on his trousers. "I'm heading to the archives before the team arrives. There are more questions I need to dig into."

Thomas nodded, fastening his belt, but his eyes never left her. There was a subtle shift in his expression, something deeper than just the conversation about work. As Elena started to walk toward the door, her mind already racing with thoughts of her next move, Thomas reached out, grabbing her by the arm.

Before she could react, he pulled her close, his hand gently lifting her chin, and kissed her. The kiss was intense, filled with the unspoken emotions and the connection they had shared the night before. It was a moment that said more than words could—their bond, their passion, and the weight of everything that lay ahead.

When they finally broke apart, breathless, Elena met his gaze, her heart pounding in her chest. Thomas gave her a small, knowing smile. "Be careful in the archives."

Elena smirked, playfully swatting him. "I will. But don't think that kiss gets you out of reinforcing the framework. You have work to do, too."

With a final grin, she turned and left the music room, leaving Thomas standing there, watching her go.

CHAPTER 17

In the quaint town that cradled the historic manor of Elena's recent fascinations lived Miriam Foster, a retired librarian with a fervour for history that extended beyond her years behind the reference desk. Her small, cosy house was a treasure trove of artefacts and old books, its walls adorned with ancient maps and photographs of historic landmarks. Since her retirement, Miriam had dedicated herself to unravelling the forgotten tales of the town's past, driven by her love for mysteries and untold stories.

Miriam's interest in the town's history began when she stumbled upon a mention of Abigail in a tattered edition of the town's chronicles at a local book sale. Intrigued by a brief footnote that hinted at a scandalous love story, she embarked on a relentless quest to uncover more. Her fascination with Abigail's story had dimmed over time, but with Elena's work on the manor, Miriam found a renewed interest and a fresh opportunity to delve deeper.

Her path crossed with Elena when the archivist gave her Elena's number, leading to an invitation to Miriam's charming cottage for coffee.

"Have you found any more letters from Abigail?" Elena asked eagerly.

"No, but I did find something intriguing," Miriam replied, her eyes lighting up. "I've been looking into their story as well. I can't believe we're finally connecting over this."

Miriam's motivation was twofold: the thrill of the historical chase and a deep belief in history's power to teach and inspire. She saw Abigail's story as a way to shed light on the struggles and triumphs of women in history, making it relevant to the present by connecting it to the lived experiences of today's residents.

Elena, seeing the value in Miriam's knowledge, proposed, "This is amazing. Maybe you can help us. My team and I are working on restoring the manor, and if you could answer some questions, it would be wonderful."

Miriam, slightly hesitant, replied, "Are you sure? I don't want to intrude."

Elena reassured her, "Don't worry. You'll fit right in. I'm curious about the town's gossip from the 18th century."

Elena took her notebook and opened it.

"Was Abigail and Samuel's relationship so scandalous that it became public knowledge?" she began, her voice thoughtful. "Were there rumours or whispers about the true nature of the engagement that were now coming to light? Was Abigail being forced into this marriage to salvage her family's reputation or to align with powerful interests?"

"My dear, I know exactly where to find those answers," Miriam said while placing her cup of tea down on the table.

In the warm and inviting atmosphere of the cottage, the discussion continued as Elena and Miriam pored over the intriguing documents laid out before them. The morning light cast a gentle glow on the rich array of historical artefacts and records.

"I look at these often. It helps me to connect with the town and those who have passed through it. It was more of a hobby at first. However, I am surprised that it has now turned into a full career," Miriam chimed.

As they settled in, the room filled with a gentle golden light filtering through the stained-glass windows, casting colourful patterns on the dusty shelves. Miriam reached into her worn leather briefcase with an air of solemnity and carefully withdrew a folder, aged but meticulously cared for. She laid it on the table, her hands slightly trembling with the weight of its significance.

Elena, eager to delve deeper, posed her questions once more. "Miriam, can you help us understand if Abigail and Samuel's relationship was so scandalous that it became public knowledge? Were there rumours about their engagement and its true nature?"

Miriam smiled knowingly and reached for a delicate, bound diary that had been carefully preserved. "I found this diary among some personal collections. It belonged to a young girl who lived in the town during Abigail's time."

She opened the diary to a page dated March 1798, revealing a handwritten account of a conversation the girl had with Abigail:

"Today, Lady Abigail Ashford spoke to me about the mysteries of physical love, a subject considered too daring for our young minds. She spoke with such passion and openness that it made me wonder about her own experiences. I overheard talk that she and a musician were deeply involved, and though many try to ignore it, it seems that everyone knows of their affair. It's the talk of the town, and even Lady Abigail herself cannot escape the scrutiny."

Elena read the passage with astonishment. "So, the affair between Abigail and Samuel was widely known. It wasn't just a private scandal—it was something that the entire town was aware of."

"Yes," Miriam confirmed. "The diary clearly indicates that their relationship was the subject of much discussion and gossip, even among the younger generation."

Elena then turned her attention to the next question. "What about the engagement? Were there any local sentiments about the true nature of Abigail's marriage to Sir Crampton?"

Miriam carefully laid out a document from a town council report dated April 1798. It was a record of workers' grievances and discontent regarding the marriage. One of the entries caught Elena's eye:

"The upcoming marriage of Lady Abigail Ashford to Sir Crampton is causing unrest among the workers. Sir Ashford's appointment to the council will enable him to vote on crucial labour issues, including work hours and conditions. As he owns multiple factories, this new position will have a significant impact on our livelihoods, and we fear it will only benefit the wealthy at our expense."

Elena's eyes widened as she absorbed the implications. "So, the marriage wasn't just a personal affair but had tangible consequences for the community. Sir Ashford's influence over labour conditions was a major concern for the workers."

"Exactly," Miriam said. "The workers were deeply concerned about how Sir Ashford's increased power would affect their working conditions and their lives."

Elena moved on to her final question. "How could Sir Ashford and Sir Crampton justify such cruelty? What made the marriage so critical that it necessitated

Abigail's suffering?"

Miriam reached for another document—a town council resolution from May 1798 detailing Sir Ashford's appointment. She laid it out, revealing the strategic importance of Abigail's marriage to Sir Crampton:

"The marriage of Lady Abigail Ashford to Sir Crampton will grant him a council seat, thereby increasing his influence over city taxes and other crucial decisions. Sir Ashford's position will enable him to affect fiscal policies and vote on important matters which would otherwise be inaccessible to him. This move is seen as a strategic advantage in consolidating power and extending his influence in the region."

Elena absorbed the information with a mix of awe and concern. "So, Sir Crampton's marriage to Abigail was not just about social alliances but was a strategic move to gain political power and control over city governance."

"Yes," Miriam confirmed, her eyes reflecting the weight of the historical context. "The marriage was a calculated manoeuvre to enhance Sir Crampton's and Sir Ashford's influence, affecting both local politics and economic conditions."

As the discussion drew to a close, Elena felt a profound sense of purpose. The documents and insights Miriam provided painted a vivid picture of the forces at play in Abigail's life, revealing the broader implications of her story.

"It's not all. This," Miriam began, her voice steady despite the obvious emotion, "is something I believe will change everything we thought we knew about Abigail." The folder contained a death certificate, the document proclaiming in neat, flowing script that Abigail Clairmont, nee Abigail Ashford, had died in France at the age of eighty-two.

The letters had given a glimpse into Abigail and Samuel's story. However, this was the first time they had seen something that wasn't told from their perspective.

Elena leaned forward, her eyes scanning the document eagerly. The death certificate was dated over two centuries ago, stamped by the French authorities in a small town that is now part of modern-day Provence. It listed natural causes as the reason for her death, and most crucially, it mentioned her long-term residence in the same town.

Miriam anticipated the questions that might arise. "I cross-referenced the birthdate listed here with the baptismal records we found last year in the church archives. The dates match perfectly. And look here," she pointed to a faded seal at the bottom, "this is the official crest of the town. I verified its authenticity with the current mayor's office in France. They confirmed it has been in use since the 17th century."

The implications of the certificate were profound. If this document was indeed legitimate, it not only confirmed Abigail's successful escape to France but also her life there—a life that spanned decades beyond the oppressive forces she had fled.

Elena's face lit up with a mixture of relief and excitement. "She really did it, then," she whispered, more to herself than to anyone else. "She escaped and lived a life of her own making."

Miriam nodded. "To think she managed all this at a time when such acts were nothing short of revolutionary for a woman."

The room was filled with a new energy, a blend of academic excitement and personal connection. They were no longer just researchers; they were witnesses to the unfolding story of a woman who had defied the constraints of her time to carve out her own destiny.

As they discussed their next steps, the trio felt a renewed sense of purpose. This death certificate was not just a piece of paper; it was a testament to a woman's resilience and a key that unlocked the deeper truths of her life story.

As the initial excitement of uncovering Abigail's death certificate settled, a new, pressing question emerged: What had become of Samuel? Miriam, with her unquenchable thirst for historical truths, took it upon herself to trace Samuel's fate, a task that proved to be as challenging as it was intriguing.

"I've looked for him for years," Miriam commented. "Unfortunately, I can't confirm anything. We can only hope that he made it to France as well."

The discovery of Abigail's long life in France significantly altered the narrative that Elena had been meticulously constructing around her story. Until now, their tale had been one of tragic love—lovers separated by societal barriers, their fates shrouded in uncertainty. The revelation that Abigail not only escaped but thrived in a new land reshaped their story into one of resilience and hope.

This change brought a wave of both professional satisfaction and emotional resonance for Elena. From a historical perspective, the evidence of Abigail's longevity and her ability to establish a life on her own terms was a testament to the agency often stripped from women of her era. It challenged the typical narrative of women in the 18th century, presenting Abigail not just as a figure constrained by societal expectations but as a pioneer who forged a new path for herself. This aspect of her story provided a powerful counter-narrative to the oppression usually highlighted in historical accounts of women's lives during that period.

Elena, who had grown increasingly connected to Abigail through their research, felt a profound sense of relief and happiness for her. She saw in Abigail's story a mirror of her own desires for autonomy and fulfilment. "To know that she lived her years in a place where she was perhaps free to be herself—it changes everything," Elena reflected one evening as they organised their findings. "It's not just a love story; it's a tale of emancipation, of the triumph of personal will."

And even if they couldn't shed the same light on Samuel, Elena hoped that he would appreciate their effort to do justice to Abigail's remarkable story.

CHAPTER 18

Elena sat hunched over a large oak table, her fingers tracing the brittle edges of ancient census records and old family trees. Each document felt like a breadcrumb in her ongoing quest to bring the past to life—the story of Abigail and Samuel, entangled in secrecy and love. Her eyes, weary but gleaming with determination, scanned through the pages, the dim light casting shadows on her face.

Across from her, Thomas leaned back in his chair, his arms crossed. He'd been unusually quiet this morning, though his presence filled the room like a heavy breath. He was watching her, his dark eyes flicking over the documents, then back to Elena, who barely noticed. She was too absorbed, too close to something monumental.

"Elena," Thomas finally broke the silence, leaning forward to rest his elbows on the table, "you've been at this for hours. What are we even looking for here?"

Her head snapped up, eyes gleaming with the same thrill she'd had the night she uncovered Abigail's first letter. "A descendant. I'm close. I can feel it."

Thomas raised an eyebrow but said nothing, watching as she sifted through more papers, her fingers moving as if guided by instinct. The room was silent except for the occasional rustle of pages until Elena let out a soft gasp. Her finger froze on a name.

"I've found her," she whispered, her voice barely audible. "A direct descendant."

Thomas stood up and moved to her side, peering over her shoulder. "Claire St. Martin," he read aloud, his voice low and steady. "From France."

Elena's heart raced as she traced the lineage with trembling hands, connecting Abigail's marriage to a string of birth records that led all the way to the present. Abigail had lived and escaped, and her bloodline survived—right up to a living, breathing person.

"Elena," Thomas murmured, his tone softer now, "this is incredible."

Her chest tightened, a wave of emotions washing over her. This wasn't just about connecting the dots anymore; it was a bridge between the past and present, a chance to touch history and bring it into the modern world.

Thomas placed a hand on the back of her chair,

leaning in slightly. "So, what's next? You reach out to this woman, hoping she's willing to open up her life to some long-lost ancestor?"

Elena swallowed, the enormity of it all suddenly weighing on her. "Yes... yes, that's exactly what I have to do." She turned to look at him, and for a moment, their eyes met in the quiet stillness of the room. His expression was unreadable, but there was a flicker of something—admiration, perhaps? Or was it simply the shared exhilaration of discovery?

"Then let's write the letter," Thomas said, his voice gentler now. "We've come this far together."

They sat side by side, the atmosphere shifting between them. As Elena began to draft the letter, Thomas watched, offering the occasional suggestion, his presence grounding her as her thoughts raced. She explained who she was, the research she'd conducted, and the significance of Abigail's story. It wasn't just history; it was deeply personal. She poured her heart into each word, determined to convey the importance of what she had uncovered.

As she wrote, she could feel Thomas's gaze on her, quiet and thoughtful. Every now and then, he'd lean in, pointing out a phrase that could be sharper or offering a softer touch where her intensity bled through too much. His input wasn't just professional—it was personal, a testament to the strange bond they had formed through this shared journey.

This was not merely a professional task but a personal

mission that seemed to weave her own life's work with the threads of lives long past. Each document on her desk was a testament to her journey into the world of Abigail and Samuel, a journey that had started as a mere academic interest but had grown into a profound quest for understanding the human stories behind the historical data.

Elena organised her materials meticulously, laying out the family trees, copies of the baptismal and marriage certificates, and her detailed notes on Abigail's life. Each piece was a building block in the narrative she hoped to share with Claire. As she sifted through the papers, her thoughts wandered to Abigail's strength and the mystery of her life after fleeing England. This connection to her descendant felt like reaching across time to touch the fabric of a lived experience, to affirm that the personal histories she studied did not vanish into the ether but continued to shape the present.

Sitting down to write, Elena felt a surge of emotion. This letter was a bridge between past and present, a way to bring closure to some of the lingering questions about Abigail's life and to open new doors for understanding the impact of historical events on individual lives. She began with a greeting, explaining who she was and the nature of her research. She was careful to imbue her writing with respect and warmth, conscious of how strange and unexpected this connection might seem to Claire.

Elena reflected on her own journey, how discovering

each piece of the puzzle had felt like uncovering hidden treasures. She wanted to convey this passion and the deep sense of responsibility she felt in sharing their shared history. She wrote about the significance of Abigail's story, not just as a tale of love and bravery but as a beacon of inspiration, showing the ripple effects of one woman's choices across generations.

As she drafted the letter, Elena included questions about Claire's family lore, wondering if stories of Abigail had persisted through the ages or if her letter would come as a surprise. She expressed her hope that this correspondence would be the beginning of a new chapter of discovery for both of them, offering to share her research findings and hoping that Claire might illuminate unknown aspects of Abigail's later life and her legacy.

Dear Claire St. Martin,

My name is Elena Carter, and I am a historian specialising in 18th-century European migrations and personal histories. I am writing to you because, through a series of remarkable discoveries and extensive research, I have traced a direct connection between you and Abigail Ashford, a woman whose life story has captivated me for the past several years.

My journey into Abigail's life began serendipitously. While rebuilding the old Ashford Manor, I stumbled upon a diary and multiple letters buried in the music room of the manor. This manuscript, penned by Abigail Ashford, hinted at a tale of escape, resilience, and, intriguingly, a forbidden love. The protagonists were Abigail Ashford and Samuel (name unknown), whose love story unfolded amid the tumultuous backdrop of political unrest and social constraints of their time.

Driven by a mix of historical curiosity and personal fascination, I embarked on a quest to uncover the truth behind their romance. My research led me to various archives and old libraries. Each document, each clue unearthed, felt like a whisper from the past, guiding me closer to understanding her life.

I am a historian through and through, and I am driven by a passion to uncover the truth that may be hiding. I can't help but feel that you are driven by a similar passion. And I hope that the two of us can collaborate together in order to find a common ground as well as some form of reprieve. Abigail's story is one that is begging to be told, and I hope you can help me tell it.

Abigail's story is not merely a tale of historical significance; it has become a profound narrative of human endurance and the power of love against the odds. It has deeply impacted my views on the intertwining of personal choices and historical events. Learning about her struggle for autonomy, her daring escape to France, and her life after that has provided me with invaluable insights into the broader themes of migration, identity, and adaptation.

Through my research, I discovered that Abigail lived a full and fulfilling life in France, where she left a legacy that, I believe, carries forward to you. This connection we share with her through time is a testament to the enduring impact of her decisions made centuries ago. It is a reminder of how the past continuously shapes our present and informs our understanding of identity and belonging.

With this letter, I hope to open a dialogue between us. I am eager to learn about any family stories or documents you have inherited about Abigail and Samuel. Any information would enrich the current understanding and add a more personal dimension to the historical records. Additionally, I would like to share with you the details of my findings and the historical context of Abigail's life, which might provide you with a deeper connection to your ancestors.

This letter may come as a surprise, and you may need some time to consider this unexpected link to the past. Please know that I approach you with the utmost respect and sensitivity to the personal nature of this history. My intention is to honour Abigail's legacy and, with your permission, to continue exploring the ripple effects of her life choices that have echoed through generations.

Thank you for considering this outreach. I look forward to the possibility of exchanging stories and furthering our understanding of a shared past. Please feel free to contact me at your earliest convenience so we can discuss how best to proceed in a manner that respects both your privacy and the significance of this discovery.

By the time the letter was finished, the room had

grown darker, the autumn light fading into evening. Elena sat back, reading the final words aloud.

Thank you for considering this outreach. I look forward to the possibility of exchanging stories and furthering our understanding of a shared past.

Warmest regards, Elena Carter.

She sighed, setting the pen down and rubbing her temples. "That's it."

Thomas nodded, a hint of a smile tugging at his lips. "It's perfect. Now we wait."

Elena sealed the envelope with care, the weight of centuries seeming to press down on the small paper. She stood, stretching, her muscles stiff from hours of tension. Thomas joined her, his arm brushing against hers as they moved toward the door.

"I'll walk with you," he said, glancing at the envelope in her hand. "Might as well make sure it gets there in one piece."

The walk to the post office was filled with an easy, companionable silence. The air was crisp, the scent of fallen leaves mixing with the distant salt of the sea. Elena felt a strange sense of calm settle over her. Despite the weight of the discovery, Thomas's presence grounded her, reminding her she wasn't alone in this journey.

They reached the post office, and with a deep breath, Elena handed the letter over, watching as it disappeared into the system. Her heart clenched with anticipation and hope.

On their way back, Thomas broke the quiet. "So, what's next? Once you hear back from Claire?"

Elena smiled softly. "Then we'll know where Abigail's story truly ends—or maybe where it really begins."

Thomas chuckled. "You know, for someone who claims to hate mysteries, you're awfully good at finding them."

"I don't hate mysteries. I just hate when they take too long to solve." Elena rolled her eyes, but there was warmth in the gesture.

"Speaking of mysteries," she began, her tone shifting slightly, "did you ever hear back from your old schoolmate? The Crampton descendant?"

Thomas exhaled, shaking his head. "No. I left him a message, but he never returned my call. I suppose he's either busy or not interested."

A mischievous glint flashed in Elena's eyes as she smiled. "Well, lucky for us, the Crampton house isn't far away. Only an hour's drive."

Thomas raised a brow, catching on to her implication. "You're suggesting we just show up at his doorstep?"

Elena shrugged, the smile lingering on her lips. "I'm suggesting we make it a little harder for him to ignore us. Besides, you can charm anyone, right?"

Thomas laughed. "I don't know if unannounced visits count as charm, but…" He paused, clearly tempted by the idea. "Alright. Let's see if he's more willing to talk face-to-face."

As they walked back toward the manor, side by side, the brisk air seemed to carry the weight of centuries with it. But in that moment, it wasn't just about the past. The future—uncertain and full of possibilities—was waiting for them both.

CHAPTER 19

The drive to Crampton Manor felt endless, the narrow country roads twisting through ancient woods and overgrown hedgerows. The sky above was a sullen grey, and a fine mist hung in the air, clinging to the car windows as they rolled up the gravel drive. The manor itself loomed ahead, a stately old house with ivy creeping over its stone facade, the kind of place where secrets seemed to linger in the very walls.

As they pulled to a stop, Elena glanced at Thomas, whose expression was unreadable. He'd been quiet during the drive, his usual easy-going demeanour replaced with something more guarded.

"You ready for this?" she asked, giving him a small smile.

Thomas exhaled, his eyes fixed on the imposing manor ahead. "As ready as I'll ever be."

They exited the car, the crunch of gravel underfoot the

only sound in the damp stillness. At the front door, Elena hesitated for just a moment before knocking. The brass knocker echoed through the heavy wood, and after a few moments, the door creaked open. A stern-looking servant appeared, his eyes flicking over the two of them with mild curiosity.

"Can I help you?" the man asked, his tone polite but firm.

Thomas stepped forward. "I'm Thomas—Thomas Reynolds. I went to Eton with Mr. Oliver Crampton. I left a message a while back."

The servant's brow furrowed slightly, but after a moment's hesitation, he nodded. "Please wait here. I'll see if Mr. Crampton is available."

He gestured for them to follow, leading them into a small, dimly lit sitting room. The air was thick with the scent of old leather and polished wood, and a large portrait of an unsmiling Crampton ancestor dominated one wall. The servant disappeared, leaving them in silence.

Elena glanced around, her fingers absently brushing against the edge of a polished table. The weight of the house pressed down on her, its history palpable in the dark wood and heavy drapes. She could feel the tension radiating from Thomas as they waited. The minutes dragged on uncomfortably.

Finally, Oliver Crampton strode in, his expression sour and his posture stiff. He was a tall man with sharp features and the kind of rigid bearing that suggested he was not used to being inconvenienced. His eyes flicked over Thomas, a faint sneer tugging at his lips.

"Thomas," Oliver said, his voice cool. "If I haven't returned your call, there will be a reason for it."

Thomas's jaw tightened, but before he could respond, Elena stepped forward, sensing the tension rising between the two men.

"We're not here to impose, Mr. Crampton," she said, her voice calm but steady. "Our visit isn't about your family, but rather the Ashfords. Specifically, Abigail Ashford."

Oliver's gaze shifted to her, the faintest flicker of interest crossing his face. He didn't reply immediately, but his eyes narrowed slightly as he considered her words.

"The Ashfords," he repeated, his tone sceptical. "And what, exactly, does my family have to do with them?"

Elena took a breath, steadying herself. "We're conducting research on Lady Abigail Ashford, who, as you may know, was engaged to one of your ancestors, Sir Crampton. The engagement surprised the entire town at the time, and we're trying to understand why. There are pieces of her story that remain unclear, and we were hoping you might have some insight."

Oliver's expression darkened, his jaw tightening. "You've come all this way, digging through ancient family history, just for some romantic gossip?"

Thomas bristled, but Elena shot him a warning glance, silently urging him to stay calm.

"It's not gossip," Elena said firmly. "It's history. Abigail's life—her choices—are a significant part of what we're trying to uncover. She was more than just someone's fiancée. There's a larger story here, one that has been buried for centuries, and we believe that story involves more than just the Ashfords."

Oliver crossed his arms, his gaze shifting between the two of them. For a moment, it seemed like he might throw them out, but then something in his expression softened—just a little. Perhaps it was curiosity, or maybe it was the way Elena spoke, her passion for history unmistakable.

"You mentioned you're trying to show what life was really like for women in the 18th century—not just as wives, but as individuals?" he asked, his tone still reluctant. "It's good that you're focusing on that. Feminism has its place, even now." He paused, then added, "But I'm not sure how much use I'll be. The records I have are pretty limited, and honestly, I've never been one to get caught up in old family gossip."

Elena suppressed a sigh of relief, nodding gratefully. "We appreciate anything you can share. Even the smallest details might be helpful."

Oliver motioned for them to follow him out of the sitting room and through a series of narrow hallways.

As they walked, Elena's mind raced, her thoughts darting between the fragments of information they'd uncovered so far. Abigail's engagement to Sir Crampton had always seemed out of place, a puzzle piece that didn't quite fit with the rest of her story. And now, standing on the precipice of what could be a significant breakthrough, she felt a familiar surge of excitement.

The huge study was cloaked in a kind of suffocating stillness, broken only by the occasional rustle of paper as Elena laid out the documents she'd carefully collected over the past few weeks. The weight of history, layered in old ink and fragile parchment, filled the air. Across from her, Oliver Crampton lounged in his chair, watching with an air of mild disdain as she meticulously arranged each paper on the desk.

"These are the key documents," Elena said, her voice steady despite the undercurrent of tension in the room. She gestured to the letters, articles, and records she had compiled. "They paint a picture of Abigail Ashford's life, of her engagement to Sir Crampton, and of the town's reaction. It was more than just a wedding—there was real intrigue surrounding it."

Oliver's lips curled into a smirk as he picked up one of the letters, his eyes barely glancing over it before he dropped it back onto the desk. "It's no surprise," he said with a dismissive wave. "The whole town was talking about it because it was astonishing. A girl of *minor virtue*—a known troublemaker who had an affair with a musician, no less—somehow managed to secure a marriage to someone of my ancestor's standing. That kind of thing gets people talking."

Elena's brow furrowed, but she didn't flinch. "That's not exactly a feminist viewpoint."

Oliver shrugged, his smirk unfazed. "I never claimed to be a feminist. But I do believe it's important for a gentleman to play the part when needed."

Elena sigh. "You're only seeing part of the story. The engagement was more than just gossip fodder. Your ancestor, Sir Crampton, may have been a nobleman, but he was far from wealthy. Monsieur Ashford was a man with ambition. By marrying his daughter to Sir Crampton, he secured himself a place on the town council. Sir Crampton may have had the title, but Ashford had the money—and political leverage to offer."

Oliver straightened slightly in his chair, his smirk fading. "Are you suggesting my family took bribes for political positions? I assure you, we didn't need to stoop to such tactics."

Elena held her ground, her eyes unwavering. "I'm suggesting that Abigail's engagement was part of a larger transaction, one that benefited both families—your ancestor gaining the wealth he needed and Ashford earning his place among the town's elites."

A tense silence fell over the room. Thomas, who had been standing by the window, turned and walked slowly toward the centre of the study. His gaze drifted downward, a slight frown creasing his brow as he studied the floor beneath their feet.

"Elena," he murmured, his voice thoughtful. "Look at this."

Elena followed his gaze, her eyes widening as she took in the intricate mosaic pattern that stretched across the floor. It was an elegant design, with swirling shapes and colours that seemed almost alive in the dim light of the study.

"It's the same pattern," Thomas said, his voice gaining strength. "The floor here—it's exactly the same as the one at Ashford Manor."

Oliver's eyes narrowed, his body tensing as he glanced down at the mosaic beneath them. "What are you getting at, Thomas?"

"This floor," Thomas continued, kneeling to trace the lines of the mosaic with his fingers, "It's the exact same as in the Ashford Manor. It's not a coincidence. This pattern—this particular mosaic—is unusual. It's too unique to be replicated accidentally."

Oliver shifted uncomfortably in his chair, his brows knitting together as he considered Thomas's words. For a moment, he seemed at a loss for how to respond, his usual confidence faltering in the face of this unexpected detail.

"I'm sure the Ashfords must have visited Crampton Manor before the wedding," Oliver finally said, his voice clipped. "Perhaps they liked the design and wanted to replicate it in their own home. It doesn't mean anything."

Elena exchanged a glance with Thomas, her mind racing. The connection between the two families ran deeper than they had thought. This wasn't just about an engagement of convenience or a political deal. The mosaic, with its intricate, almost symbolic design, hinted at something more—something shared between the Ashfords and the Cramptons.

How hadn't I noticed this before? Elena thought to herself.

Elena remained silent for a moment, her gaze locked onto the mosaic underfoot. Her fingers traced the edge of one of the tiles, and slowly, she looked up at Oliver with renewed determination.

"Did you know," she began, her voice calm but charged with intensity, "that the Battle of Culloden took place in 1746, just fifty years before the engagement between Abigail Ashford and Sir Crampton?"

Oliver glanced at her, his expression stony, but something flickered in his eyes—whether curiosity or irritation, Elena wasn't sure.

"It's not just a random detail," she continued. "After the Jacobites were crushed at Culloden, the 1770s and 1780s saw the gradual rollback of the oppressive laws that had been passed in the wake of the rebellion. By 1792, most of them were lifted when the Catholic and Episcopal clergy began to pray for the monarch again.

But not everyone let go of their loyalties. The Jacobites didn't fade into obscurity; they remained."

Oliver folded his arms, clearly unimpressed. "And this relates to my family's history how?"

Elena took a slow breath, her eyes narrowing as she stood. "In 1798, Henry Stuart was still fighting for his rights, still rallying people to his cause. He was eventually given a small annuity by George III—four thousand pounds a year. A pittance, dressed up as an act of royal charity."

Oliver's expression wavered, but he held his ground. "Again, I don't see what this has to do with—"

"It has everything to do with this," Elena interrupted, pointing to the floor beneath them. "Look closely, Oliver. This mosaic—it's not just decorative. This motif," she said, crouching to touch the centre tile, "is a white rose of York. It's cleverly hidden, I'll admit. But it's there."

For a moment, no one spoke. Oliver's face darkened, his jaw clenching as he stared down at the tiles. He knelt beside Elena, squinting at the intricate design. His fingers hovered over the swirling patterns, suddenly seeing them in a new light.

"The white rose," Thomas murmured, realisation dawning in his voice. "A symbol of the Jacobites."

Elena nodded, her voice calm but unwavering. "The Ashfords and the Cramptons were aligned with Jacobite sympathies, weren't they? Maybe not openly, but subtly—hidden in their homes, their alliances, their politics. Abigail's engagement to Sir Crampton—it wasn't just a strategic marriage to solidify power. It could have been part of a larger, secretive allegiance to the Jacobite cause. This floor—this symbol—it connects them to a rebellion that didn't die with Culloden."

Oliver's face twisted in a mix of disbelief and frustration. "That's ridiculous. My family has always been loyal to the Crown."

"And yet," Elena said softly, "this floor tells a different story."

The tension in the room thickened, and Oliver stood abruptly as if putting distance between himself and the unsettling revelation beneath their feet. He rubbed a hand across his mouth, his eyes flicking between Elena, Thomas, and the mosaic as though weighing whether to dismiss it all or confront a truth he'd long avoided.

"You're playing with fire," Oliver muttered, his voice low. "This is dangerous territory—one that could ruin reputations, destroy legacies."

Thomas crossed his arms, his expression measured. "Come on, Oliver, my family was Jacobites, and we are still lairds. It's been two hundred years and multiple slaughters. The truth has a way of surfacing, no matter how long it's been buried."

Elena rose to her feet, gathering her documents with

a sense of quiet purpose. "We're not here to ruin anyone, Oliver," she said firmly, her voice steady but not without sympathy. "We're historians. We seek the truth, not to disgrace a family, but to understand what really happened. Abigail's story has been buried for too long. We have a responsibility to uncover it."

Oliver hesitated, glancing once more at the white rose embedded in the mosaic. His defences wavered, and for a moment, his face softened, revealing something beneath the bravado—a hint of uncertainty, of long-buried knowledge scratching to the surface.

Oliver sighed, rubbing the back of his neck as if finally surrendering to the weight of the past. "My family never talked about this. Most people thought the Jacobites had been wiped out after Culloden, but that was not totally the case, especially not in this region. Everyone knew—secretly, of course—that Jacobite sympathisers still existed. They didn't flaunt it, but it was there, in the alliances, in the subtle symbols."

Elena and Thomas shared a glance, the final piece of the puzzle coming into view.

"And Abigail," Elena said quietly, "was at the centre of it, even though she had no idea."

Oliver leaned back, crossing his arms over his chest. "Yes, but not by choice. She didn't care about any of that. It was her father and Sir Crampton who orchestrated everything. They thought the marriage would unite the Jacobite factions in the region, strengthen their hold, to gain more influence in the town and maybe even make some noise for Henry Stuart's cause. But when Abigail ran away, it all fell apart—or at least the alliance did."

Elena took a deep breath, thinking over the significance of what they had uncovered. "We're not trying to stir up old wounds, Oliver. We're planning an exhibition focusing on the role of women in history, particularly in politics—how their choices were so often limited, yet how they still played crucial roles in shaping events."

Oliver looked at her, his defences dropping slightly as the purpose of their visit became clearer. "You're saying Abigail's story would be part of that?"

"Exactly," Elena said. "It's not just about the politics—it's about her, too. Her choices, or lack thereof, that reflect the limitations placed on women of her time. We want to show the personal impact of those larger movements."

Oliver hesitated for a moment, then turned to a nearby desk drawer. He rummaged through it and pulled out a folded piece of paper. The corners were worn, and the ink had faded, but the document was still legible. He handed it to Elena with a reluctant sigh.

"This," Oliver said, "is a copy of a letter between Sir Ashford and my ancestor, Sir Crampton. It was written just before the engagement was announced. The letter suggests that the marriage between their children would help unite the Jacobite supporters in the region. It's not much, but it confirms what you're saying."

Elena carefully unfolded the letter, her eyes scanning the faded words. Sir Ashford and Sir Crampton had indeed plotted to use the marriage as a tool to bind the Jacobite sympathisers, using Abigail as a pawn in their game. It was heartbreaking and fascinating at the same time.

"This is exactly what we needed," Elena said softly. "Thank you, Oliver."

Oliver nodded, though his expression remained grim. "Just be careful with this information. Even after all these years, some people don't take kindly to their ancestors' secrets being dug up."

Thomas placed a hand on Oliver's shoulder. "We'll handle it respectfully. We're here for the truth, but we won't tarnish anyone's legacy unnecessarily."

Elena folded the letter carefully and slipped it into her bag. She glanced around the room one last time, taking in the lingering tension in the air. The truth they had uncovered was more than just a forgotten family feud—it was a window into a world where politics, rebellion, and personal choices collided in ways that still echoed centuries later.

As they prepared to leave, Oliver's voice stopped them. "You've got your answers. Just make sure you tell her story right."

Elena smiled, her eyes full of determination. "We will."

As Elena and Thomas prepared to leave, Oliver's voice stopped them.

"And also, write my name as a donor. In big enough letters. It's great to be a feminist these days."

CHAPTER 20

The morning of the grand opening was a blur of activity. The team buzzed around the manor, ensuring every final detail was perfect, adjusting displays, and guiding the first wave of visitors through the carefully curated spaces. Elena moved from room to room, nerves fraying at the edges. This was the moment they had all worked so hard for, and its weight pressed down on her shoulders like a heavy cloak.

In the dining room, Sophie made sure the timeline display was flawless while Aarav and James double-checked the lighting in the room. Clara was coordinating with the press at the entrance, but even her efficiency couldn't stop the slight tremor in her hands. Everyone felt it—the pressure, the excitement, the fear of something going wrong.

Elena stood in the library, staring at the Jacobite flower floor, her mind racing. She couldn't stop thinking about the tiny details, all the what-ifs and the maybes. What if the lights failed? What if the sound in the music room didn't sync? What if people didn't understand the story they were telling?

She hadn't noticed Thomas approach until his hands gently rested on her shoulders, his fingers massaging the knots of tension at the base of her neck. "You're going to drive yourself crazy," he murmured in her ear.

Elena let out a shaky breath, grateful for the small reprieve from the tension winding through her body. "What if something goes wrong?"

"Everything is perfect," Thomas reassured her, his voice calm and steady, the opposite of her racing thoughts. "And if something doesn't go exactly as planned, no one will notice but us."

She gave a small nod, trying to believe him, but her shoulders were still rigid with stress. Sensing this, Thomas leaned down and pressed a soft kiss to the back of her neck, just below her hairline. "Relax, Elena. You've done an amazing job."

Before she could respond, he turned her to face him. With a tenderness that caught her off guard, he kissed her in front of everyone—right there, in the middle of the library. It was their first public display of affection, and for a moment, the world seemed to stop.

Elena's heart fluttered, the weight of her worries melting as Thomas held her close. When they broke apart, she noticed the rest of the team had gathered nearby, their faces alight with surprise and delight.

Sophie was grinning from ear to ear. "Finally!"

James let out a low whistle. "About time."

Even Clara, always composed, was beaming. Aarav gave an exaggerated thumbs-up, which sent a ripple of laughter through the group. Elena felt her cheeks flush, but the warmth of Thomas's arm around her shoulder grounded her, reminding her that, despite all her fears, this day was a celebration.

The stress she had carried for weeks seemed to evaporate in that moment, replaced by a sense of calm and joy. The manor was ready, the team was united, and they had done it together. And now, with the public streaming through the doors, Elena could let herself breathe.

The opening of Ashford Manor was a resounding success, with the public turning out in droves. Thanks to Moira's extensive media coverage, which alerted the entire village, and, surprisingly, Oliver Crampton's efforts—clearly eager to position himself as a man of value—the buzz around the event had reached far and wide. Visitors streamed in, curious to see the restoration and discover the secrets hidden within the manor's walls.

The Whispering Room captivated them immediately. As soon as they stepped inside, they were transported back to 1798. Soft, haunting music from the era filled the air, creating an ambience that felt both intimate and mysterious. Shadows moved across the room, shifting in a subtle play of lights as if lovers were hiding in secret corners, whispering to one another just out of sight. The effect was mesmerising, and the room's quiet magic left visitors in awe.

Guests paused, their voices hushed as they observed the interplay of light and sound. The atmosphere felt almost otherworldly, as if they had stepped into a moment frozen in time. It was as though Abigail and Samuel's forbidden love story was unfolding right before their eyes, whispered through the music and shadows.

Elena stood back, watching the scene unfold with a sense of pride and satisfaction. The transformation of the music room into this immersive experience was exactly what she had envisioned—an enchanting space where history comes alive, not just in facts and figures, but in emotion and mystery. The visitors were drawn in, captivated by the magic that lingered in the air, making the moment unforgettable.

Elena stood in the grand dining room, watching as visitors moved through the space with quiet excitement. Sophie's talent had truly shone, but in a way no one had anticipated. Her elegant menus, originally crafted for the manor's events, had been repurposed as a creative timeline for the history they've uncovered. Each menu sat beside articles, newspaper clippings, and letters, all carefully arranged to unravel the mysteries of Ashford Manor.

"Elena, look at them," Thomas murmured beside her, his voice low but full of pride. "They're eating it up."

She smiled, watching a group of visitors huddled around one of the tables, pointing at a letter, debating Abigail's scandalous love affair. "I can't believe it's all come together like this," she said softly, her voice filled with wonder. "It feels surreal."

Visitors paused in front of the displays, snapping photos and whispering excitedly as they connected the dots between Abigail, Samuel, and the secrets that had long been buried within the manor's walls. The dining room had become a hub of discovery, the past coming to life through these carefully curated details.

"And this is just the beginning," Thomas said, motioning toward the open doors leading to the library. "Look."

Elena followed his gaze as people made their way into the library, where a challenge awaited them. The restored Jacobite flower floor, intricate and beautiful, hid a clue within its design—a detail that held the key to understanding the deeper layers of Abigail's story.

"They're searching for it," Elena said with a grin, watching as some visitors crouched down to study the floor, their expressions intent. "I love this part. Some of them will get it, others won't."

"That's the beauty of it," Thomas added, slipping his hand to her lower back in a supportive gesture. "They'll keep coming back, trying to figure it out."

As they watched, a small group of teenagers huddled together, pointing excitedly at a section of the floor. "I think they found it." Elena laughed. "They've solved it."

Thomas chuckled softly. "Smart kids."

The sound of footsteps echoed through the hall as more visitors ascended the grand staircase, their phones raised to capture the polished marble bannisters and the soft light flooding through the windows. Every step up the staircase was met with awe as people took selfies and panoramic shots, ready to share their experiences online.

"I didn't expect social media to explode this fast," Elena admitted, pulling out her phone and opening Instagram, where posts tagged with "#AshfordManor" were multiplying by the minute.

"That's the thing about this place," Thomas said, his voice filled with pride. "It's a perfect blend of history and spectacle. People love it."

Elena turned toward him, her heart swelling with a mix of relief and joy. "I wasn't sure it would resonate with people like this."

Thomas stepped closer, his hands finding her shoulders as he began to gently massage away the tension that still lingered. "You knew. You've poured your heart into this place. It's no wonder people are connecting with it."

Elena sighed, feeling the tightness in her muscles

slowly ease. "I guess I didn't know it would feel this overwhelming."

At the heart of the grand unveiling stood a plaque, a small but significant addition to the manor's new identity. At Oliver Crampton's request, the plaque was installed to honour the contributions made during the research that had brought the manor's hidden stories to light. It bore two names: Miriam Foster and Oliver Crampton.

For Miriam, the moment was pure joy. As she stood before the plaque, her eyes gleamed with pride. Her love for history, deep curiosity, and contributions had been immortalised within the walls of Ashford Manor —the very place that had captivated her imagination for so long. Seeing her name etched into the metal felt like a culmination of her passion, and she couldn't help but smile at the sight. Being part of this project and seeing Abigail's story come to life was more than she had ever dreamed.

Oliver, on the other hand, was far from pleased. As he approached the plaque, his face darkened. He had expected to be honoured, certainly, but not like this. His name, sharing space with that of Miriam Foster—a retired librarian, a commoner, in his eyes —was nothing short of an insult. He had requested recognition, but not at this level. It was a blow to his pride, and he stood there, staring at the plaque with a mixture of fury and disbelief, feeling as though the legacy of his prestigious family had been diminished.

Elena, observing from the side, couldn't help but find the situation somewhat ironic. Here was Oliver, so insistent on maintaining the grandeur of his lineage, now brought low by a simple plaque. But Miriam's beaming face, radiant with happiness, made it all worth it. This moment was about more than just names on a wall—it was about the collective effort, the blending of past and present, and the power of shared stories.

As the last visitors filed out of Ashford Manor, leaving behind the echoes of laughter and whispered conversations, Elena took a deep breath. The day had been overwhelming, exhilarating, and emotional. She watched as the team wrapped up, exchanging smiles and high-fives, the success of the event written all over their faces.

The manor felt different now—alive with the stories of the past, yet vibrating with the excitement of what had been achieved. Elena's mind raced, thinking of all the small moments that made the day a triumph, but she also felt an odd sense of calm settle over her.

"Quite a day, huh?" Thomas approached her, his voice warm and reassuring. He slipped his hand into hers, giving it a gentle squeeze.

"I still can't believe how well it all went," Elena replied, her smile soft but genuine. "It's everything we hoped for."

Before they could fully reflect on the day, two representatives from the Historical Society of

Scotland approached, their expressions serious yet pleased. One of them, a woman with sleek hair and a polished demeanour, spoke first.

"Elena, may we have a word?" she asked, motioning toward a quiet corner of the manor. Thomas raised an eyebrow but released Elena's hand as she nodded and followed the pair.

As soon as they were alone, the woman spoke. "First of all, congratulations. The opening was a tremendous success. We've been watching closely, and it's clear that the public response has been incredible."

"Thank you," Elena said, her heart racing slightly, unsure where the conversation was heading.

"We came to discuss something important," the other representative, a man with a sharp gaze, chimed in. "We believe Ashford Manor has the potential to be more than a temporary exhibit."

Elena blinked, taken aback. "More than temporary?"

"Yes," the woman continued. "The story you've told here—the narrative of power, love, and secrets, framed through the lens of women in history—resonates deeply with modern audiences. It's not just a historical curiosity; it's a conversation about power and the roles women have played, often behind the scenes."

The man nodded. "We want to offer you a proposal. We believe Ashford Manor should become a permanent museum dedicated to power and women as tools of power—women like Abigail, whose stories have often been overlooked or misunderstood. And we want you to lead it."

Elena's heart skipped a beat. "Me? You want me to...?"

"Under your leadership, the museum could continue to explore the intersection of history, feminism, and influence," the woman explained. "We see you as the perfect curator for this project. Your passion, your connection to the manor, and the story you've brought to life—it's exactly the kind of vision we need."

For a moment, Elena was speechless. The weight of the offer, the responsibility, felt immense. But as the words sank in, she felt a surge of excitement and pride.

"I—I don't know what to say," Elena stammered, glancing at the now-quiet manor around her. "This is... beyond anything I could have imagined."

"Take your time to think it over," the man said with a smile. "But we believe this is the perfect next step for Ashford Manor. And for you."

As the representatives left, Elena stood in the fading light of the manor's grand hall, the enormity of the offer swirling in her mind. This could be the start of something far bigger than she ever dreamed—an opportunity not just to preserve history but to shape its retelling for future generations.

CHAPTER 21

Elena and Thomas were in their shared office, surrounded by the familiar chaos of books and papers, when the long-awaited letter from Claire St. Martin arrived. The morning sun filtered through the window, casting a warm glow over the piles of research that had defined so much of their lives together. As Thomas handed Elena the envelope —a thick, cream-coloured paper sealed with a simple yet elegant wax stamp—there was a moment of weighted silence filled with anticipation.

Elena turned the envelope over in her hands, her fingers tracing the contours of the seal, feeling the imprint of history in its ridges. The weight of the paper carried the weight of the past, each fibre interwoven with the narrative they had dedicated years to uncovering. "This could be it," she whispered in her voice, a mixture of excitement and reverence.

Thomas watched her with a supportive smile,

understanding the magnitude of the moment. "Go on," he encouraged, his curiosity equally piqued by the contents that awaited them.

With careful hands, Elena broke the seal and unfolded the letter. As she read the opening lines, her expression transformed—a mix of relief and joy bloomed across her face. Thomas, unable to contain his curiosity any longer, leaned in to catch a glimpse of the words that seemed to bring such a profound response.

The letter began with Claire expressing her gratitude and excitement at connecting with them, followed by a heartfelt recounting of Abigail and Samuel's story as passed down through her family. She confirmed not only their successful escape to France but also the life they managed to build together—an affirmation of the tales that Elena and Thomas had pieced together from fragments and conjectures.

Elena looked up at Thomas, her eyes gleaming with tears of joy. "They made it, Thomas. They really made it," she said, her voice thick with emotion. The letter in her hands was more than just paper and ink; it was a bridge across centuries, a confirmation of a shared history long buried but never forgotten.

Together, they sat down to pore over every word, each line a thread in the rich tapestry of Abigail and Samuel's enduring legacy. This letter was not just a piece of correspondence; it was a historical document in its own right, one that would add a profound layer of depth and authenticity to their research.

Claire's letter unfolded with a narrative both vivid and evocative, chronicling the life Abigail and Samuel forged together after their daring escape to France—a tale of love, resilience, and clandestine success against the odds.

"Dear Elena and Thomas," Claire wrote, "I am thrilled to provide you with details that have been passed down through generations in my family, albeit often whispered as if the echoes of the past could still bring about repercussions. After Abigail and Samuel escaped the oppressive constraints of their native England, they found refuge in a small but vibrant village in the south of France. Here, amidst the rolling vineyards and burgeoning artistry of the era, they began anew, under the veils of pseudonyms that allowed them the freedom they so desperately sought."

Samuel, known in France as 'Monsieur S. Clairmont,' reinvented himself as a musician. "Samuel's music," Claire detailed, "became his voice, through which he narrated tales of loss, love, and liberation. His compositions, infused with the pain of exile and the sweetness of newfound freedom, resonated with many and soon earned him a following that spread far beyond the confines of our quaint village."

Abigail, too, found her own form of expression, supporting Samuel's career not only as a loving partner but as his muse and occasionally his manager.

"Abigail wrote in one of her letters," Claire quoted, "'in our music, we have found both a sanctuary and a stage, a means to inscribe our lives in the annals of this new land that promised us liberty but demanded its own sacrifices.'"

The letter went on to describe their modest prosperity, the challenges of living under assumed identities, and the bittersweet freedom they experienced. "Though they were far from the persecution that once shadowed their every step, the weight of their past was never fully lifted," Claire wrote. "Their love, however, remained their fortress. Abigail often expressed in her diaries how that love was the melody that sustained them, the rhythm that propelled them through their darkest days."

Claire's recounting also touched upon the local legend that Samuel once performed before an assembly of notable composers and musicians of the time, his identity still cloaked under his pseudonym. "It was said," Claire recounted, "that the applause that night was thunderous, a symphony of acceptance and acclaim for a composer whose true history remained as enigmatic as his melodies."

The letter concluded with Claire expressing her hope that the information she shared would enrich Elena and Thomas's understanding of Abigail and Samuel's lives. "May their story," she wrote, "serve as both a testament to the enduring power of love and a reminder of the sacrifices so many have made in the pursuit of freedom and fulfilment."

Elena and Thomas, deeply moved by the letter, felt as though they had uncovered a treasure, the true legacy of Abigail and Samuel not just preserved but celebrated in their descendant's words—a story of triumph not only over societal constraints but also over the confines of time itself.

Printed in Great Britain
by Amazon